THE DRAGON PRINCE

Ghostspeaker Chronicles Book 5

PATTY JANSEN

GET FREE EBOOKS

Visit pattyjansen.com
to sign up for Patty's mailing list. You get four series starter
ebooks for free!

CHAPTER 1

THE CLANG OF A GONG echoed through the hallway of the palace, a strange, foreign-sounding noise that made the hairs on the back of Johanna's neck stand up.

In slow, deliberate strides to the low beat of a drum, the visiting party from the ship of the eastern traders entered the Red Reception Room.

Upon hearing of Li Han's intended visit, Johanna had made sure that the room, unlike the rest of the palace, was in a state suitable to receive and impress a foreign visitor. For the past few days, a small army of people had been scrubbing the floor, polishing the chairs and fixing patches in the patterned wallpaper. They had gathered any furniture they could find that didn't have fire or water damage, and selected the cleanest rugs and the freshest, least damaged curtains.

But the group of people that came through the door looked so splendid that all that effort seemed akin to trying to dress up a donkey as a coach horse.

First came two mountainous soldiers in grey uniforms

carrying a wooden chest on a platform with handles on both sides. From the way they walked, Johanna—seated on the ornate but otherwise quite ordinary chair that functioned as makeshift throne—judged that whatever it contained had to be heavy. They progressed about halfway into the room, set down their load, bowed in unison and retreated to both sides. Behind them came two soldiers in leather armour. They wore the same grey shift and loose trousers as the porters—Johanna judged them to all be guards. They also bowed and stepped aside.

This allowed Johanna to see the elderly couple in the middle of the group. The old man was dressed in a blue robe. He was finely built, quite short and thin in comparison with the guards. His weather-beaten skin displayed a landscape of wrinkles and sunspots, especially around the curiously shaped eyes. He had tied his greying hair in a bun at the top of his head.

Next to him stood a woman of similar age with a wizened face. Her hair was more white than grey and also tied at the top of her head. Her face was round, and she looked around the room with eyes narrowed to slits. She wore a knee-length robelike garment woven from shimmering green silk and a broad embroidered belt around her waist, with trousers of the same colour.

Women wore trousers?

The young man behind them was much taller. He wore simple black with leather armour over the top. An empty scabbard hung at his waist. Like the soldiers, he had left his weapons at the door.

Behind him were two more soldiers and then four people with an assortment of curious-looking drums. One of them carried the gong, a big metal disk suspended from a frame.

The entire party came to a halt and bowed as one. The

gong made a soft noise as it swung against the side of the frame.

The old man said in a strongly accented voice, "We bow to the king and queen of Saarland and the dignified people of the King's Council."

Those wise men of the council, including Father, sat to Johanna's left. The king, of course, wasn't present, not even in spirit. He was in the garden chasing frogs. Father had even taken his chair away to save Johanna the embarrassment of having to explain his absence.

Johanna said, "I return your greeting. Rise and tell us your names and your business in our fair town." Her hands felt sweaty and the smell of polishing wax that hung around her chair made her feel ill.

The old man straightened. "My name is Li Han, brother prince of the Dragon Emperor. This is my wife Wen Mei and my son Li Fai. The Dragon Emperor, my brother, has sent us here to trade. We bring silk and spices, cloth and beads. Tobacco, cocoa, tea. Everything from all parts of the known lands and from the lands at the edge of the southern ocean. We buy cheese, wool, rugs, wood products, baskets, furniture. We trade with Phoenicians, Anglians and the tribes of the western horn. We trade all over the known world and explore the unknown world. Today I bring my son, Li Fai. He wants to make office in this city." He gestured to the younger man in black, who again bowed, his hands pressed together in front of his chest.

When he straightened, Johanna met his eyes. They carried a sharp, intelligent expression. His skin was bronzed, his lips full and dark.

She said while returning his gaze, "So you want to have an office in Saardam?"

His father replied. "Yes. Office. Warehouse. We bring

goods. We sell them. River traders bring them to all the river towns. They take other things back for us to buy. Cloth, shoes, cheese. We buy them and sell elsewhere. People of Phoenicia really like cheese." He glanced at Father as he said that. Father of course had met Li Han before during his years of travelling on the river sloops. He would speak of meeting him in Lurezia where the river was deep enough for the sea traders to come a good distance inland if the wind was right.

"We have our own sea traders in Saardam," said Joris Decamp, mayor of the city and in charge of all matters dealing with the seaport. "They will not like foreigners coming in, taking their positions."

There were some nods at this in the King's Council, the group of twenty men at Johanna's left. Apart from Father and Master Deim and the shepherd of the Church of the Triune, most of them were nobles wearing their brocade and silken finery.

Someone at the back of this group said, "The Nielands could use a kick up the backside, if you ask me. Yes, we have sea traders, but they still haven't done anything about rebuilding the ocean ships they lost. Tea is getting mightily scarce. I say let him have his office." This was Hendricus Franzen, and Johanna made a mental note of his comment.

"Old Nieland will not like that at all," repeated Joris, and that comment met with some approval.

Johanna licked her lips. What Li Han asked was no small thing. Before the fires, the Nielands had a good fleet of seafaring vessels. Many of them had been destroyed in the fire, one had never returned after a mutiny and the rest were damaged, but nevertheless, the family must be planning to repair and rebuild those ships. Li Han was a major competitor.

Johan Delacoeur cleared his throat and asked Li Han in

his usual blunt manner. "Never mind the tea, spices and trinkets. They're women's things. What I'd be interested in is this: do you sell those iron ships of yours? Because there would be a long line of people wanting to buy them."

It became very quiet in the room. Everyone was keen for the answer to the question.

Li Han bowed to Johan. "We do not sell ships. We sell goods. We use ships. If we sell ships then we cannot trade anymore." He chuckled, not entirely convincingly. He had to be aware of the failed efforts of various groups in the lowlands to try to build their own iron ships, and the fact that a war had been fought over control of the port because of these ships.

Johanna asked, "If you get an office, are you going to bring more iron ships into the harbour?"

"We may. Or we may not. In the future. Not now."

Johanna glanced at Father. Did Li Han just sound coy or was he actually coy? Not wanting to reveal if this was their only ship or if they had more than one?

Father smiled at her. Well that was most unhelpful. She could use some help in deciding what to do about this delegation.

Johanna said, "One of the problems with your request is this: many people in town are suspicious of the iron ships. They are afraid and don't understand why they can move without sails."

That was an understatement. Ever since the ship had come into the harbour, rumours had run rife about the motivations of the eastern traders, the size of their fleet hiding in a secret location waiting to pounce on Saardam and occupy the city, and also about the size of the fire dragon that—according to many—lived in the belly of the ship.

Li Han bowed again. Was he going to keep doing that

every time he said something? "The people do not need to be suspicious. The idea for the iron ships came from someone from this part of the world. One of your countrymen made the first drawings for the steam machines. His name is Rinius. He is a man of great ideas."

"Rinius is a heretic!" called Shepherd Victor from his seat in the King's Council. "It is not just the Church of the Triune that considers him so. Even the Belaman Church—and they're not usually known for making wise decisions—have condemned him. He was banished to a small island off the coast of the Cape, and hanged there."

Li Han said, "Your king speaks well of Rinius."

There was a small uncomfortable silence after this.

Yes, Roald rarely shut up about Rinius and his books. It was one of the reasons that no one was keen to pressure him to come to meetings anymore. But how did Li Han know this?

A couple of men in the King's Council were keeping an eye on the shepherd; others suddenly found their knees very interesting. The outburst they feared from the shepherd did not follow, however.

Li Han continued as if oblivious to the tension, "If we have office and warehouse, we will pay the sons and fathers of this town to work for us."

"Do you think we have no work for our own men?" This was Johan Delacoeur.

The shepherd said, "Do you think our citizens will want to work for someone with magic who supports the greatest heretic of all time?"

Thomas Kloostermans, a fervent supporter of the Belaman Church said, "Yeah. I don't usually agree with him, but that man wrote a great many things that are an insult to any church, not just his—" He glanced sideways at the shepherd. "—band of lunatics."

The shepherd called out a protest at the same time as Johanna said, "Gentlemen."

They fell quiet.

That was the division in the city: those who supported the Church of the Triune and those who said it had gained far too much power.

"The eastern trader's office in our town will be an opportunity for all involved, but . . ." She met Li Han's eyes. "I'm afraid that a number of our buildings are not in a very good state. Quite a few were damaged by fire. Many were abandoned, and we may not be able to trace the owners to transfer a lease or ownership. Other buildings are damaged beyond repair."

Li Han nodded. "We can fix. You find building. We pull down and build or fix. We bring gold to pay for office."

He said something to the two mountainous guards in his own language. It sounded sharp and unpleasant.

The guards lifted the lid of the chest that still stood on the platform in front of the delegation.

Gold indeed, in the shape of coins.

There was so much of it!

Johanna still remembered the shock of walking into the king's vault when she and Roald moved into the palace and looking at the empty shelves. Somehow she had expected there to be at least some money.

Father had talked about how King Nicholaos had given a fortune to the Church of the Triune when he believed they could resurrect his daughter the crown princess Celine, and when they couldn't, to the necromancer Kylian. In panic, the king had wanted to sell his only asset—his child-like son who was utterly unsuitable for the throne—to the richest merchant's daughter to raise money. Somehow, though she'd known all that, she still hadn't realised how bad it was until she looked in the treasury.

And now the family's only hard asset—the palace—had been looted and damaged in the fires.

Johanna had already borrowed money from Father and Master Deim for the essential repairs, but she didn't want to accept too much of their generosity, because she didn't think the palace would be in any kind of position soon to pay back the loan.

Li Han's money would go a long way towards solving her problems.

If she let Li Han's son have his office.

Noticing her hesitation, the eastern trader's son took a handful of the coins and crossed the room holding them on his open palm. While he came to Johanna, she met his eyes. They were black and the shape of them was unusual but not unattractive. The rest of his face was pleasant to look at, his lips expressive, his nose broad and quite flat, not at all like the big honkers that people from the south often had. His skin had a slight yellowish tinge and was soft like that of a girl. He had no beard or moustache. His hair was black and glossy like a raven's feathers. He wore it tied at the top of his head.

He bowed and held the coins out to her. She took them. The skin on his hand was pleasantly warm and dry. His nails were neat and clean.

"It is Phoenician gold." His voice was warm, not as heavily-accented as his father's. Johanna made a show of examining the sample of gold. The coins were very heavy and carried a foreign inscription on one side and a likeness of some god on the other. Of course Johanna had seen these before. Many deals with foreigners were paid for in Phoenician gold. "Yes, I have no doubt that they're real."

She gave the coins back to him, again touching his palm. He tossed them back into the chest with a clink.

From inside his cloak, he produced a parcel wrapped in a

silk cloth. "To show our appreciation, this is a personal gift to you." He handed the parcel to her. Johanna had to struggle to keep meeting his eyes. His expression was so intense and she didn't know why he looked at her like that, whether that was customary where he came from, but the intense gaze made her ears burn. She didn't want to stare back because that would be inappropriate. She heard that in some foreign lands morals were very loose.

Johanna laid the cloth on her knees and unwrapped it, glad for the distraction. The fine fabric slid through her hands. If these people used silk to wrap things, they must be very rich indeed.

Inside the parcel she found a piece of honey-coloured wood carved into a long-tailed creature. It had a big snout with two large, open nostrils. Its mouth was open, showing a forked tongue.

"It's a dragon," he said. "This is the blue dragon. It is the symbol of our house. It's a present to you."

"Thank you. It's very pretty." Johanna traced the exquisitely carved scales on the dragon's back with her fingertips. "You speak our language well."

There was a brief flash of a smile in his eyes. "I have studied much. The office will be mine while my father travels on the ship. I have to make deals with traders in your town. I cannot expect them to know my language."

"No, that's true."

He chuckled. Had he attempted to make light-hearted conversation? "Maybe one day I can teach."

"Yes, maybe. Thank you," she said again, aware that the men of the council were looking at her.

He bowed and retreated.

By the Triune, her cheeks were burning. He had magic of some kind. There was no doubt about it.

But what about his request for an office?

She wanted to accept it.

In the past, Saardam had always been an accepting place, where people from all walks of life and parts of the known world had come together.

If someone was going to dominate the sea trade on which Saardam's wealth had relied in the past, it would be those with iron ships. It could be the eastern traders, who already had the iron ships, or the Baron, who had not succeeded in building them yet. Even without knowing Li Han well, she knew who she'd rather deal with. Father was an infallible judge of character and he had always spoken well of the eastern trader.

Yes, there was probably magic involved in the building of a successful iron ship.

Yes, many people in town would view him as a major competitor.

Yes, allowing him to settle would bring a war with the Baron a step closer simply by keeping Saardam independent.

A little voice inside her said, *Wasn't this war going to happen anyway?* Because the baron did not just want to use the port, he wanted to erase Saarland from the map. He wanted to kill the royal family and eradicate its church.

Wouldn't Li Han be a powerful ally against the Baron and his necromancer son?

"This request takes me by surprise, but I'm quite interested in your offer. I would like some time to consider possible offices that you could occupy."

There were several gasps in the King's Council. One of the men made a protesting sound, but another shushed him.

Li Han bowed. "Thank you, thank you. We come back in a few days, right?"

"Yes. Do come back." There was a seed of an idea forming in her mind but she needed a bit of time to work it out.

"Thank you, thank you." He bowed again.

The two mountainous men picked up the chest of gold and Li Han and his party shuffled backwards to the door, leaving behind a thick silence. The gong sounded again when they were in the corridor.

Johanna did not dare look at the men to her left.

CHAPTER 2

A S SOON AS the eastern traders were gone from the room, several of the powerful men in the King's Council raised their voices.

"That was a rash and irresponsible decision. You cannot know what hidden motives they have for coming here," Johan Delacoeur said. His face went red, as it usually did when he was agitated. "A lot of people will be very angry."

"Those people can have their say," Johanna said. "I will listen to their arguments. I have not given him my word, only that I'm interested."

"With all due respect, Your Majesty, is that decision up to you alone? I don't think so." When Johan said *all due respect* he usually meant no respect at all.

"According to our agreement, only the king can make that decision without support from the council," another noble said.

There was some murmuring of agreement at this. Apparently a young woman who was not from a noble family was such a threat to them that they needed an entire council to keep an eye on her.

Johanna found it hard to meet Father's eyes. He and Master Deim were in the minority. *They* didn't think that she was incapable of making decisions, but the council had been one of the conditions under which the noble families had accepted the "Idiot King" on the throne.

It was a fragile agreement for a fragile position. They couldn't afford arguments.

"I cannot see why we can't rebuild our own ocean trade," a man said.

"We don't need foreigners to run business for us!" another shouted.

Another man said, "I agree. These foreigners and their gold are likely to take our best workers away from us."

"Then pay them more!" Master Deim said.

"Gentlemen!" Johanna's voice cut through their arguments. "Like it or not, we face the reality that, underneath our veneer of sophistication, Saardam is struggling to overcome the effects of the past. The invasion and occupation by Alexandre have sucked the city dry. We have no food until harvest, and not enough people are left on the farms who know how to work the fields."

"We can buy food," Johan Delacoeur said.

"Yes, but many of the poor will not be able to afford it." Not to mention that the coffers were empty.

He snorted. "They can survive off bread and water. Entire armies do it. For surprisingly long periods of time, too."

Master Deim spoke up. "The poor are those who provide the workers to rebuild the city, as well as the quay workers, the ones who unload and load our ships. Prosperity of the land is not measured in the wealth of the rich, but in how many of the poor can afford to feed their families. Because if they can, they're happy. They won't steal, they won't join rebellions. Give a poor man a job and pay him, and he will happily work for you."

"That's just what these eastern buggers are trying to do, isn't it?" That was the noble Thomas Kloostermans. "Get a foothold in the city and spread their foppish ways and foul religions. I mean—which man lets his wife wear trousers, for the sake of the holy god."

"Not many of you are old enough to remember the last time that happened," said Patricius Faber, a man easily the oldest of the council. "When preachers of this ludicrous church came into the city and subverted our merchants and workers with notions that they are somehow equal to nobles. The next thing, the king himself was taken with this rubbish, having had his senses clouded through the loss of his daughter. And no one stopped him, and we were all saying 'I told you so.' Twenty-five years on, our *women* are going to this church and are begging us to come. This church has corrupted the core of our civilisation. That's what will happen when you let foreigners in. First they give our workers jobs, then they buy things from our merchants, and then they attempt to corrupt us by appealing to the weak minds of our women."

Johanna was very much tempted to say, "Well, maybe then you should do something that those people will find worth supporting instead," but she had no energy for an argument.

Johanna shifted in her seat. She needed to get up and out of this room, because the corset made her uncomfortable. It pushed her stomach down so that her front was flat. But that expanding waist had to go somewhere. It was all squished up inside. She had to take shallow breaths because there was nowhere for her lungs to expand.

If she got up, the men would see that the dress sat wrong and that the bottom of the bodice wasn't done up at all. But, by the Triune, she was feeling unwell all of a sudden.

"If you're asking me, Your Majesty, the man's gold is

bewitched," Shepherd Victor was yelling over the other voices.

A couple of the men protested.

"Look at how it makes you fight like little children. He showed you the gold and now you're all fighting over it. This man is a magician. He is using magic to befuddle our minds and cloud our senses. It was evident from the way you all looked at him. Especially Your Majesty was affected by his foul tricks of magic."

Johanna bit her lip. Arguing with him achieved nothing except cement the opinions of these men against her. Women shouldn't be leading countries. If she'd still been alive, Celine would have had to rule under a King's Council, too.

"I'm sorry, but I don't think it's in our interest that the church keep insisting on banning magic," Master Deim said. "We need magic in Saardam, even if only because everyone else uses it. It would be stupid not to teach any magic and not to attract people who know magic. When you keep banning magic, the people with magic will leave, and next time a magician like Alexandre comes, we'll be defenceless."

That was already happening. Loesie had left town two months ago. She'd said she needed to look after her grandmother's farm, but surely the increasing hostility towards magic had something to do with it.

The shepherd spread his hands. "It's not up to me to decide what is allowed or not. The *Book of Verses* says that magic is the work of the Lord of Fire and we should not get involved with it. It says in the Book of Truths: 'The man who attains his wealth through any other than the work of his hands shall be punished.' "

"That's not about magic. That's about stealing."

"Stealing and magic and other devious methods. It's all the same. Money makes good men forget their morals."

Johan Delacoeur snorted, "How easily did the church accept the king's money when he was offering?"

"The church never accepted coin," Shepherd Victor said.

"Small detail. They accepted the gifts that the king bought with money. That's the same in my language."

"The Triune teaches us to refuse the money that is given in return for favours and accept the gift given from the good-will from a person's heart."

Master Deim said, "Oh, stop that nonsense argument. When you're poor and someone wants to give you something, you don't care if it's coin or goods or why it's given. It doesn't matter. The man pays for a service or he pays because he expects a favour."

And then other men from the King's Council joined in, debating whether accepting goods could still be considered bribery and whether the trader's generous offer of gold for the use of an office could be considered a bribe.

Some said it was and some said that if you held people to that standard, none of the powerful men passed muster, and then someone else said that maybe they needed different people in power. Within moments, they were all shouting at each other.

Johanna sat back in the chair. She really had to get out of here soon.

"Gentlemen." Johanna raised her voice. By the Triune, her head was swimming.

They fell quiet, glaring at each other.

"Bickering achieves nothing. I have no doubt all of you are well aware of the position of the city and the royal coffers. There is no money. Our citizens need money. The trader's money would solve many of our problems."

"It is tainted money!" the Shepherd Victor called out. "Tainted by magic. Bewitched. Designed to twist our minds."

"Rubbish!" Johan Delacoeur shouted back. "It's money. Gold coins. What's the magic in that?"

"Everything can have magic. Water, air, fire, wood, metals . . ."

"Gentlemen!" More forceful now. She rose.

"Tell me that metals can't have magic and I'll be quiet," the shepherd said, looking directly at Johanna. "Since Your Majesty seems to know all about magic." The expression on his face disturbed her. It was almost a madman's.

She would have said something, but her vision went blurry. She sat back hard on the chair, almost missing the seat.

Someone far off said, "Your Majesty?"

Johanna lifted her head, looking at Master Deim. His face was swimming in and out of focus.

"Are you all right? Do you need to lie down?"

Father was rushing towards her, too.

"I'm fine," Johanna said, but her heart was thudding. "Just a bit tired. It's very hot in this room."

"Let me take you to your private quarters." Master Deim offered his arm.

Johanna took it and he pulled her up. Her knees felt like they'd give out on her any moment.

"Are you all right?" His voice sounded concerned.

"Yes, I was just . . . it's too hot in this dress. We will continue with our normal meetings tomorrow," she continued to the assembled members of the King's Council, trying to school a business-like tone in her voice. To the mayor, she said, "See to it that the eastern trader gets shown possible accommodation for his business premises. I want to make sure that he doesn't go elsewhere while we decide."

Joris Decamp bowed. "I will, Your Majesty."

She let herself be guided to the hallway on Master Deim's

arm. Father followed them. No one said anything until they were almost at the king's private quarters.

Then Master Deim said, "It's come to my attention that you don't appear to be as astute as you usually are. I've watched you today, and you're distracted, irritable and you keep touching your stomach. Is there something you're not telling us?"

His grey eyes were penetrating. There was no hiding it any longer. "Yes, I'm with child."

"My goodness. We must take steps to secure the kingdom."

"I've already done that." Father had insisted that she sign the scary documents about what should happen in case of her death in childbed.

"You must see a nurse regularly."

"I'm seeing Helena."

"Helena. You mean the southern whore?" He gave her a horrified look.

"She can't see customers anymore, with her face disfigured through the fire. I trust her. She has a lot of experience with women's matters."

"I bet she does." He didn't sound entirely convinced. "When can we expect a little prince or princess?"

"Helena says in late summer."

"That's not very far away." He ran a disturbed glance over her tightly-laced bodice that hid the increasingly obvious signs of her condition. "You should be resting."

"There is no time for resting."

She didn't *want* to rest, because her thoughts would drive her crazy if all she could do was sit and do embroidery and worry about what she would do if it was all too obvious that Roald was not the father of this child.

Because he was not, she grew ever more certain of that. Back in Burovia, in the farmhouse that belonged to the

Guentherite Brotherhood, Kylian had bewitched and poisoned her and had in one act done what Roald had been unable to do in many.

Sometimes when she lay in bed, she could feel the child's magic flow through her lower body.

They entered the king's private sitting room, which faced the garden. Sunlight flowed in through the windows. There were a couple of books on the couch, but Roald was nowhere to be seen. He was probably in the garden catching frogs or drawing butterflies.

Johanna took the books off the couch and sat down. Father sat next to her.

"I hope you know what you're doing by suggesting that Li Han will have his office," Master Deim said.

"I don't, but I am familiar with the alternative because we've just lived through it. I figure that the eastern traders couldn't be any worse than Alexandre. For one, they're interested in money, not occupying us."

He nodded, but didn't look convinced. "I'm more worried about what the Baron will do when the eastern traders and their ship settle here."

"That's why I need to talk to you about an idea I have," Johanna said.

The men both looked at her.

Johanna began, "We have no money, but we have something everyone wants: our seaport."

"Yeah, well, that's what all this is about," Master Deim muttered.

"And the iron ships. If Li Han stays, we have those, too."

Master Deim nodded. "And the iron ships."

Johanna continued. "We can defend Saardam, but however successful we may be at protecting ourselves, Saardam will always remain a place that countries and royal families will fight over. Those who control the port decide who comes in and what they sell. At certain times, countries or families will get upset over this and they will send men like Alexandre."

Father raised an eyebrow as if curious where this was going.

"There are a great number people who want control over Saardam. They fight over magic or no magic, over this or that church, over ideals and beliefs and royal families. But at the end of the day, they would probably settle in favour of having a good relationship with those in control of the port. They will choose cooperation over a war. I'm also guessing that they will not wilfully harm—like set fire to—assets that are partially owned by their country."

Father gave her a sharp look. He seemed definitely both puzzled and intrigued now.

"I'm proposing that we form a cooperation of all those who have an interest in our port. I'm proposing that we send an official letter to all lands that have interest in Saardam. Places like Burovia, Gelre, Estland, all the areas along the rivers that are accessible through Saardam. Some will be friendly to us, some won't. We will tell them all the same thing: with their help, we will rebuild the harbour and provide services to transport goods inland and we'll have facilities where their traders can sell their goods so that their countries can prosper as well as ours."

"Yes, but we always had something like that. . . ." Father frowned.

"Then we tell them the next bit: Saardam has been destroyed and we need investment. We create investment allotments that they can buy, at a certain value each. In return for their money we give them favours, or if they can't use those favours because they never visit the city, we pay a return on their investment. We make up contracts for different levels of investment."

Father lifted his hand to his chin as he always did when he needed to think about something.

Master Deim said, "That's an interesting idea, but what does this have to do with the eastern trader?"

"Li Han? It's easy: he will be one of the biggest investors. He wants an office, so we give him an abandoned warehouse and he pays to fix it up. We get his business, and keep an eye on his iron ships. And because we don't want to be seen favouring just him, we offer the same service to others."

"I don't know that it will work," Father said.

"Trying to keep out certain groups of people certainly won't work," Johanna said. "The people who get banished, disowned or mistreated will band together and they will attack us when we seem weak, because they don't like Roald on the throne, or they don't like the church, or some other reason. That's what happened with Alexandre. King Leo and Baron Uti have an unlimited number of cousins they can send. All of them probably have magic. They're watching and waiting, making up the next excuse to invade us. Whether it's Li Han or the church or some other reason, it doesn't matter."

"Well . . ." Father said.

"I think it's a very good idea," Master Deim said. "The question is: will the stubborn King's Council allow you to carry it out? You need their support, unless Roald can make a convincing case for his support of the plan."

Johanna let her shoulders sag. The latter was never going to happen, and making the King's Council support her was an impossible task.

"I have to try." There was no alternative except continued wars and murder, including that of Roald, herself and her child.

CHAPTER 3

WHEN FATHER and Master Deim were gone, Johanna asked the maid to tell Nellie to see her in the dressing room.

Johanna went down the corridor to that room. The damage from fires and subsequent flooding was extensive and had left marks almost everywhere: wallpaper was peeling, floor tiles had come up, dark stains marked the walls and all of the king's beautiful furniture had been stolen, leaving her and Roald with old things from the attic that were often also water-damaged.

There was no money to buy new furniture and no money to fix the damage. Most of the groundsmen were working for the palace in exchange for a roof over their heads and food in their bellies, but they received no pay.

The dressing room held only a row of wardrobes in which Johanna had collected all the clothes that she had salvaged from her own house and Queen Cygna's bedroom. Compared to Queen Cygna's dressing room, it was a very poorly appointed affair. Queen Cygna would have had at least a mirror, a dressing table with matching chair and a variety of items like clothes racks that seemed a luxury until you didn't have them, because you couldn't possibly leave a precious dress on the floor.

As it was, the room didn't even contain a small table for the tea and cakes that the maid had brought. The tray stood on the floor.

Nellie came in very soon after Johanna.

"You called for me?"

"Please let me out of this dress, Nellie."

Nellie went to Johanna's back, and her nimble fingers started unlacing the bodice. Johanna breathed in shallow breaths.

The dress came off. Nellie hung it over the wardrobe door with a rustle of velvet. It had belonged to Queen Cygna. It was pretty, but Johanna wouldn't be wearing it anymore.

Then the corset. Nellie started at the bottom and with each hook Nellie undid, a little shiver of relief crept up Johanna's spine. Just how tight it had been became evident when Nellie took the corset off. Johanna was overcome by a sudden wave of nausea when all her insides went back to their normal places.

"It *was* very tight. You were right, mistress. You are becoming so big. You must get the modiste to make you some special dresses."

"How about I'll do without the corset? That gives me a bit more room in the dress."

"Mistress Johanna, you can't possibly do that. What will people say?"

"No one will notice if you do the bodice up tightly. But it will be much more comfortable for me. I never used to wear corsets much when I lived with Father."

"That was different."

"Why?"

"To start off, you weren't a queen. You weren't a married

woman. You were always far too much of a tomboy." Nellie counted off on her fingers.

Johanna sighed. "Yes, well, I have to go to church now and I'm not wearing the corset."

"But—"

"I'm not wearing it."

Nellie sighed. "Well, if you insist. But you should really get the modiste—"

"That's not going to help me for tonight."

"No, but if you would just stop being so stubborn, it might help you tomorrow. You have the little one to consider. How would you like being so squished up in there that your mother can't even breathe properly, let alone eat? For what reason?"

"You don't understand, Nellie."

"I understand well enough. If you don't look after yourself, you'll regret it later. You're going to be a mother. You should take things easy. You're going to grow and grow, until you won't be able to hide it anymore. Why hide it anyway? The people are going to love it, because they're sick of bad news."

Nellie was probably right. The people of Saardam would love it. There had not been a royal birth since Celine, despite the Queen's young age—she had been seventeen when Celine was born.

The problem was not the people. It was the King's Council.

"Which dress do you want to wear to church, Mistress Johanna?"

Johanna cut through the fog of her thoughts. "The brown one, thanks, Nellie."

Nellie helped her step into the dress and pulled the heavy material over her underdress. She then started doing up the lace at the back of the bodice.

Johanna gasped. "Not so tight at the top." Her breasts were swollen and very tender.

"I know." Nellie worked her way down, pulling the lace as she went.

"It's too tight," Johanna said.

"I can't make it any looser. The lace isn't long enough."

"Then make the lace longer. Just don't make it so tight around here." Johanna pulled the bodice down over her stomach. It pushed the bump of her stomach flat. Johanna ran her hand over the front of the dress. It was very, very tight.

"Pardon me for saying this, but you're very stubborn," Nellie said. "Look at yourself in the mirror. Doesn't that look like a woman with child? How long do you think you can hide it?"

Johanna looked. Everything about her dress looked tight. Her bosom was about to burst out, the mid-section bunched up in the area between her bosom and her stomach.

Without the corset, she looked like a poorly-made sausage.

Yet she didn't want to announce her condition officially. As soon as she did, the King's Council would insist that she retire from all her duties. She did not think that Father and Master Deim alone could prevent the council making any stupid decisions. They certainly would not be able to carry out her plan for a cooperative of investors without her. They might get one or two nobles to support them, but they simply didn't have the numbers.

"Just do it up as much as you can. I'll wear a cape over the top," she said to Nellie.

"You should celebrate your condition. Otherwise you will have a child one day and people won't have known about your condition and they will wonder if the child is even yours."

"As soon as I let people know, the powerful men will want

to push me aside because they will say that I can't do my duties."

"But Mistress Johanna, you are already doing your duty. You are going to give birth to the heir to the throne."

She met Nellie's eyes. There was not a shred of humour in them.

"You should be proud. You'll have seen already that it's not an easy task."

Johanna mumbled some half-hearted comment. Memories of having to hurry out of meetings with some lame excuse because she needed to vomit were not far from her mind.

But a fear grew inside her, along with the parasite child that kept taking more of her energy.

She'd taken a peek at the sparse references to childbirth in Roald's books, and had not liked what she saw. Did a midwife really ask the woman to take off all her clothes? Did the woman really lie on a bare bed with her legs spread so that everyone could see her private parts? Was there really so much blood? Apparently other women, ones who were not supposed to be the queen, invited their friends and sisters along to give support, but, having no sisters, Johanna was too ashamed to say that she had never attended a birth. Now she was afraid to ask, afraid that it would make her more scared.

That dreadful fear of shaming herself, the fear of blood and the fear of pain was gradually taking over from the fear that someone would know straight away that the child wasn't Roald's. Because they wouldn't, at least not at the beginning. All newborns were pink, hairless worms. And ugly.

Why, again, had she wanted this?

Nellie managed to lengthen the lacing and that made the dress less tight. She also took the cape out of the wardrobe. "People are still going to ask questions if you always wear it."

"I will announce it, Nellie. Don't worry about it."

Nellie draped the cloak over Johanna's shoulders. "Normally, that happens when the child has quickened."

"Yes. I'll announce it then." But she had felt the first movement two weeks ago. "Are you finished with me?"

"You are so impatient, mistress. Church isn't going anywhere. Let me look at your hair first."

Finally, after Nellie had re-pinned Johanna's hair, she left the room. Whoa. That dress still felt tight. Tomorrow, she promised herself. Tomorrow she was going to ask a modiste to make new clothes for her.

She collected two royal guards in the hallway.

"Time to go to church, Your Majesty?"

"Indeed." Their cheerful smiles made her feel tired.

The guards accompanied her across the forecourt to the coaches. Her personal driver waited there, while the stable boy brought out the two white horses. Johanna would rather have walked, but she had found that a certain level of ceremony was expected from the royal family, and as such royals did not walk through town.

It was annoying and the church was only a short distance away, and Johanna would have walked to prove that she could, and to feel that independence that she had forgotten to enjoy when she was just Johanna Brouwer.

But today she was happy to ride, because that dress was very tight and her stomach kept hardening.

The coach took off through the palace gates.

On the main market square, a temporary church had risen from the muddy building site where Alexandre had planned his monstrosity of a building for the Belaman Church.

The trenches that had been dug by prisoners for the foundations of the building had been filled up with soil. The shepherd had put up a wooden building over the top. It was only temporary while plans for a new church were made, but the new church building should be plain, the shepherd had said, and it should be built around the statue of the Triune that the king had ordered made and that the bandits had removed from the palace garden and had been dredged from the bottom of the harbour.

As Johanna alighted from the coach, churchgoers on the steps into the entrance watched and cheered. The wind whipped up and blew strands of hair into Johanna's face.

Even if she had no wind magic, the feel of it on the air was strong.

The tree that trapped Alexandre stood downwind in the market, its twisted branches reaching for the sky. Earlier this week, it had sprouted leaves, but they had grown twisted and mottled with white from the anger of the spirit trapped inside. Every time Johanna walked past, she felt a chill, a voice calling out to her to touch the tree and read its terrible history. And every time she had to keep telling herself not to give in to its call.

Johanna went up the wooden steps of the church, flanked by the guards. As she took the top step, she felt something rip in the left side of her dress.

By the Triune, what was that?

With all these people around, she couldn't feel up there to check, but it felt like part of the bodice had come loose, because cool air stroked her skin where it shouldn't. She pulled the cloak closer around her. Something had also happened to her skirt, because the hem dragged over the ground. It got in the way of her feet and she had to be careful not to step on it.

The pews were full of people: the merchants, the workers, the mothers, the common people. A murmur of voices preceded Johanna down the aisle.

"Glad to see you, Your Majesty."

"You're looking well, Your Majesty."

"Good evening, Your Majesty."

People bowed and curtsied. Johanna walked down the aisle, clamping her left elbow to her side in case the skirt of her dress decided to come undone even more.

She arrived at the front of the church, where a row of pews was left unoccupied especially for her. Johanna sat down, flanked by the guards.

She pulled the sides of the cloak over her knees and reached up her left side under the cloak. The entire seam on that side of the dress had come apart.

This was so embarrassing. How could she make it back out of here? She could already hear Nellie berate her, *You should have a modiste make special clothes for you.* Yes, she should, but she hated standing still with people draping fabric over her and putting pins in. But there was no other option, unless she planned on going naked until the child was born.

A bell rang. People stopped talking and turned to the front of the church. The Shepherd entered from behind the altar. He wore a cream-coloured silk robe with plain red lapels. His head was bare, with his blond hair tied at the back of his head. The only piece of jewellery he wore was a gold chain with the triangle of the Triune on it. He raised his hands. He began the service with the usual words.

"Citizens of the fairest city in all the known worlds. Let us come together and celebrate the love, the fairness and the judgement of the Triune. Let us pray."

He spoke of destruction and rebuilding, of looking after the weaker people in the community. When he worked for Father, Johanna had never known that the timid accountant was such a mesmerising speaker. People listened, they hung onto every word, repeated soundlessly what he said.

His words moved from looking after each other to defending the city against threats.

"These people, they came to our town, tried to stamp out our church and our people with their filthy magic." He balled his fist. "We stood up against them. We drove them out of our town. When we stand together, we stand strong. When we stand together, the Triune will guide us. Together we will drive the magicians from the city. We pray to the Holy Father, the spirit and the ghost."

People shuffled onto their knees, hands clasped in prayer. Johanna should get on her knees, too, but she was scared that the dress would rip further, and it had to hold out for a little longer because she did want to speak to the Shepherd after the service. She didn't kneel, and found him watching her not just while she was not kneeling but throughout the rest of the service.

When the shepherd had finished preaching, people waited for Johanna to leave the church, but she told her guards that she would be staying back, so people started leaving. Johanna rose, carefully holding the ripped side of the dress by pressing her elbow to her side while keeping it hidden under the cloak with the other.

The shepherd bowed to her. He'd been preaching so vigorously that drops of sweat pearled on his forehead. "Your Majesty, I am happy to have deserved the honour that you pay me a visit."

Johanna glanced at her guards who were directing people away from where she stood. "Can we talk like old times?" Like when he was Master Willems and worked in Father's office.

He flicked his eyebrows in his oh-so-serious face. His face had aged noticeably since he had taken on the role of shepherd.

"I need your help. The whole city needs your help."

"I am forever in the service of my flock and my city and my queen." He bowed. "Tell me what you desire from your humble servant."

She thought she'd asked him to speak normally, as in old

times. Then again, he had always been distant to her. With his new position, his aloofness had only increased. "I know that and thank you. I need your support for the decisions made by me and the King's Council."

He gave her a sharp look. He was part of the council after all. "I will support anything that does not go against the teachings of the Triune."

"Going against the Triune includes denying the eastern trader the building that he would be paying for? Does the Triune teach against that?"

Another sharp look. "The Triune teaches us to stand against the menace of magic—"

"There is no evidence that the eastern traders have any magic."

"That ship of theirs! Is that not evidence? Is it not enough that the people who have tried to build these machines are all dead? Isn't it obvious that some magic ingredient is needed to make it work?"

"We know how the machines work. They boil water in a vat—"

"Only to have the vat explode and kill everyone. All those people insisted that the writings of the heretic whose name I will not mention were simple instructions for building the machine. But it is more than obvious: we are missing an ingredient of magic."

"Then we find someone with this magic if that is indeed true. What Master Deim said is true: we cannot stand against evil magic unless we have magical help. The Red Baron and his necromancer son—"

"Aiyyeee! Do not say words like that in this building! Triune have mercy." He clamped his hands together and looked at the ceiling in prayer.

A bit shaken, Johanna continued, "The Red Baron and his

son are waiting to pounce on us. They have control over . . . magical beings. The Belaman Church—"

"Aiyeee! Do not speak the name of that evil institution!"

Johanna continued forcefully, "The Most Holy Father has banished the Church of the Triune from his institution. He now considers us an enemy organisation. His church allows magic. They foster magic. They *teach* magic!"

He had clamped his hands over his ears.

"Listen to me. You can't make magic go away by ignoring it."

"Do not speak in here about the work of the Lord of Fire."

"Not all magic is evil. You should know that. It is about how you use it. Magic exists. People *will* use it. We must make sure it's used for our good—"

He turned his face to the ceiling and chanted, "There is nothing good in the deeds of the Lord of Fire. There is no salvation in his teachings. There is no redemption unless we renounce it. The strangers will unleash their fire dragons as soon as we show any sign of weakness. Do not speak to me of this terrible thing that brings us evil. Do not think of it."

Spit flew from his mouth. His voice grew ever shriller. He clamped his hands in front of his chest.

Whoa. Johanna backed away. What had gotten into him?

He sprinted across to the statue of the Triune, that same one they'd fished out of the harbour. It still showed gouges where it had been dragged and carried stain from the remains of algae and barnacle encrustations. He dropped to his knees on the wooden kneeling bench in front of the statue, wailing that the Triune should protect him from evil magic and that he would do three laps on the church crawling on his knees to cleanse the holy building of the evil that had been invoked today. His shrill voice echoed in the cavernous space.

CHAPTER 4

JOHANNA WAS SO taken aback by his outburst that she didn't even think of berating him for having spoken to her like that. When he was still the accountant Master Willems, he had always ruled in Father's office. He was a couple of years older than she was, so his authority seemed natural to her, never mind that she now ruled him. This whole concept of being queen unnerved her. It made her angry, too. She spent most of her life kicking against habits and "proper" behaviour, only to succumb to pressure by others when it really mattered. Even when she was younger, she might have protested, but in the end she did what Father wanted. She went and had a dress made, she went to the ball, she danced with the prince.

And now look at her.

She was a pawn of those men with their powerful friends and their money.

A *real* queen would order those nobles to do what she wanted. A *real* queen would never tolerate this silly King's Council in the first place.

A *real* queen would yell at her guards to give the shepherd ten lashes for saying what he had said to her. She shuddered at that thought.

She left the shepherd sitting on his knees and praying aloud, glad that he had never come to Duke Lothar's castle, Florisheim or the Guentherite farms where real magic and ghosts lurked in every bush. He would have been beside himself.

She made her way down the aisle of the church, where the church boys were already blowing out candles now that the service was over and most people had left.

The boys appeared quite calm under their master's outburst.

One of the boys bowed at her. "Don't worry, Your Majesty, he will calm down."

"Does he scream like that often?" Did her face show her unease so much that even a boy could see it?

"He does, Your Majesty." He nodded. He was a blond lad, very skinny. "He drives off the bad spirits that threaten all of us and lead us into temptation." He curtsied. "Your Majesty. You are second only to the Triune itself. We are your servants."

Johanna had no idea what to say to that, so she made a lame smile, stood back and watched him snuff the candles.

They were good candles, too, made from wax, not tallow, and they didn't smoke. Like everything else in town, wax was scarce and the candles had probably cost a small fortune. Obviously *someone* in the church had money. More money than the palace.

Second to the Triune or not, Johanna was glad for the darkness. When she continued down the aisle, she trod on the hem of her dress, and the fabric she was holding in place slipped from her fingers. Something said *crack* and cool air flowed over her exposed side through her thin underdress.

She managed to scramble into the coach, but by the

Triune, she would have to stop somewhere to fix the damage because there was no way that she could walk like this from the forecourt up the stairs, through the foyer in the palace—where there were always lots of people—and down the corridor and past the guards who stood there. There were always lots of people about and everyone was always watching her, especially the maids.

Where could she check the damage and make a quick fix?

Father's office.

As fas as she remembered, some of her knitting work was still in a basket in the corner of the reception room. It would be very dusty and might smell of fire, but there should be a needle in the basket, even if it was a fat and blunt one, and maybe she could thread some wool through the edges of the split seam so that she could at least walk without attracting too much attention.

She notified her guard that she needed to pick something up at the office and he spoke to the driver.

The coach set off through the dark streets. The horses' hooves went clack-clack on the cobblestones. Most of this part of town had been damaged by the fires, but there were signs that the families who had some financial reserves were starting to rebuild. Ruins had been cleared, materials delivered, foundation work started. Workmen had broken down the remains of burnt walls, chipped the stones clean of mortar and stacked them neatly for reuse.

In fact there were so many piles of building material in the street that the driver had to go slow to pick a path between them.

Occasional pedestrians shouted greetings. "Good evening, Your Majesty!"

The coach with the white horses had become synonymous with the queen under Queen Cygna.

Johanna waved at the window, although it was probably too dark for people on the street to see her in the cabin.

The coach stopped at the quay, in front of the steps to Father's office. The guard opened the door.

"Do you want me to go first and light the lamp?" he asked.

"Yes, please."

He went inside and lit the oil light on the shelf in the hallway with the flame from storm light that hung from the coach's driver seat.

Johanna managed to clamber out of the coach and to the door without tripping over her loose skirt. She scrambled inside and pushed the door shut.

She took off her cloak to investigate the damage.

By the Triune, the whole side of the dress had come apart. It was an old garment, but there was no reason it should have happened other than that it had been much too tight and it had not been up to the task normally reserved for a corset. With the split seam, part of the skirt had come loose, too, and it was those folds hanging down that caused the dress to drag over the floor.

But did she have anything here that she could use to fix it? She carried the lamp into the reception room, but couldn't see the basket with her abandoned knitting things. She went into Father's office at the front, where she found it on top of the bookcase. It was indeed dusty, but there was a needle and some wool. The wool was thick and not suited to sewing, and it was hard to push the fat needle through the fabric and pull the wool through without breaking it. Johanna only managed a few coarse stitches. They were so ugly they would give Nellie nightmares, but at least they stopped the dress unravelling further. It would have to do. By now, her fingers were so cold she could barely hold the needle. It had been a long time since anyone had lit the fire in this room.

Father did not use the office very much anymore. He'd

taken up a room in the palace to conduct his business. He still owned only the *Lady Sara*, and it never ventured far from port. These days, it made a lot of small trips around the local farms.

Through the cobwebbed window, she could see the coach waiting in the pale moonlight.

Behind it, Li Han's ship lay dark and menacing in front of what remained of the warehouses. A faint light burned on the deck, but otherwise there was no sign of the many crewmembers who were on board. The ship had no mast, but a fat chimney from which smoke belched when it moved.

The dark shape next to it was the *Lady Sara*—wait, what was a person doing on the deck of the *Lady Sara* in the dark? With a torch, no less?

Johanna flung the basket back onto the top of the bookcase, blew out the lamp and went outside.

The coachman and guard were waiting for her.

"Let's go home, Your Majesty. It's going to be very cold tonight."

"In a moment. Can you go and check out what a man is doing on the deck of the *Lady Sara*?" she asked the guard.

"Certainly, Your Majesty." He bowed and walked down the quay. His footsteps echoed in the stillness.

The glow of torchlight on the deck had disappeared. Johanna climbed on the coach driver's seat, but couldn't see it from there, either.

Had the person extinguished the torch when he heard people? Maybe he had gone down in the hold, whatever he was doing there. He was without a home and had nowhere else to sleep? He wanted to steal things? He wanted to set fire to the ship?

She hadn't heard Father speak of any unloading activities today. If it ever happened that the ship needed to be unloaded at night, there would be a lot more people.

Johanna waited, her heart thudding.

Her breath steamed in the glow from the light that hung on the front of the coach. One of the horses snorted.

The guard's voice rang out over the quay, followed by the sound of someone running, a thud as the guard jumped onto the wooden deck and then a big splash.

By the Triune!

Johanna climbed down from the driver's seat and made her way along the waterfront to where the *Lady Sara* lay as fast as she could without running.

"What was that?" she called to the guard on the ship's deck. At least she hoped that the man standing on the deck carrying a burning torch was the guard.

"Seems like an intruder, Your Majesty. Found this torch in the hold."

By the Triune, had this man tried to set fire to the ship? "What was he doing there?"

"No idea."

"Is there any damage?"

"If there is, it's not major. We'll have to wait until daytime to be sure." He jumped from the deck onto the quay.

By now, another person was coming down the quay from the other direction, carrying a light on a stick that swung to and fro with his footsteps.

An accented voice said, "Is there a problem?"

Li Fai.

He carried a kind of storm light, with a frame that held finely-woven silk that glowed in the light of the flame inside. The orange glow barely lit his face with those strange and fascinating dark eyes. He bowed. "We meet again, Your Majesty."

"There was an intruder on my father's ship," Johanna said.

"Our guards said they heard a shout and a splash. That was why I came to look what is going on."

"The intruder fell or jumped in the water."

"Can he swim?"

"I have no idea. I don't know who it was."

They peered wordlessly into the inky blackness of the harbour. A breeze whipped the surface into little waves that lapped at the quayside. If there was someone swimming in the harbour or climbing out further down the quay, the sounds would be impossible to hear above the singing of the wind in the ropes and the slapping of rigging against the masts.

"I did not see or hear anything," Li Fai said. "But the ducks did. They were nervous. They are never nervous for nothing. That's why we keep them on deck. As soon as they hear something, they go quack-quack-quack—"

He did such a good imitation of duck quacks that Johanna couldn't help laughing. "You have ducks aboard the ship?"

"Ducks, pigeons, parrots and a cat."

She restrained a chuckle. It was like an animal park.

"If you don't believe me, I can show you. But not now. My parents have gone to sleep."

"Sorry. I wasn't laughing because I didn't believe you, I was laughing because of the duck noise you made."

He smiled. "I spend a lot of time on deck with the ducks. I learn their language." His eyes twinkled with mirth.

"You mean it's boring out at sea?"

"It's never boring when you have ducks."

What an odd conversation. She searched his face for signs that he was having her on, but only succeeded in attracting his dark-eyed, penetrating, intense gaze. By the Triune, what did he mean by looking at her like that? Her cheeks glowed.

"I'm serious about a visit to the ship," he said. "I understand that people are afraid of it. We are happy to show our friends. But not now. At daytime."

"I would love to, thank you." She didn't think anyone, not even Father, had been invited aboard the metal ships.

"I will send an official invitation."

"I'll look forward to it."

He bowed. "Tonight, I will ask our guards to look out for thieves and trespassers."

"Thank you."

Li Fai returned to the ship with his swinging lantern. Swish, swish, swish down the quay and swish, swish, swish up the gangplank.

Johanna waited around for a bit more while the guard walked along the quay looking for signs that anyone had climbed out of the water, but he found nothing.

The cold was starting to bite, and Johanna returned to the coach. When she got back to the palace, she would send a few guards down here to help keep an eye on the quayside and the ships.

The *Lady Sara* was a precious relic of the glory of Saardam before the fires. They'd lost the *Lady Davida* and the queue at the shipyards for new ships was long.

The precious few other ships in the harbour were the sad remains of Saardam's large trading fleet. They had lost so much and could not afford to lose any more ships.

CHAPTER 5

IT WAS ALREADY quite late, and Johanna managed to slip into the palace unnoticed by anyone except the guards. She even managed to avoid Nellie and her inevitable *I told you so* speech about her ripped dress. Likely, Nellie had already gone to bed. There was always so much work to be done, and not enough people to do it. Poor Nellie.

Johanna tiptoed into the royal bedroom.

The bedroom, where no one except she and Roald and Nellie came, was one of the poorly-appointed rooms in the private wing of the palace. It contained a large bed, a dressing table with a cracked mirror and two chairs and little else.

At least it was warm.

The fire burned low in the hearth. The heavy curtains that covered the window and a door onto the balcony resembled a set of ugly rags. Nellie had washed them when they first moved in, but some of the dark mould stains would probably never come out.

Roald lay on his stomach on the carpet in front of the dying fire and was engrossed in drawing something with his brushes on a sheet of paper. He had placed an oil lamp on the floor next to him—Johanna forgot how many times she had reminded him not to do this—and a box of brushes and paint, and a bowl with water to rinse the brushes stood to his other side. Johanna came up behind him until she could see what he was drawing: a ladybeetle.

The subject of the drawing lay on a gold-rimmed royal breakfast plate and was quite dead. Its legs stuck out at a strange angle that didn't allow it to sit belly down, but Roald's drawing showed it crawling on a leaf in exquisite detail.

"I like it," she said. "It looks like it could just walk off the page." Getting no reaction from him, she walked around him and sat down on the rug facing him.

He kept drawing.

"It's very pretty," she said again.

Roald never responded to compliments, so she continued, "The eastern traders came to visit today. They want to set up an office at the quayside."

Now he looked up. The glow from the fire made his grey eyes look golden. "I must ask Li Han to bring me some exotic creatures from his travels."

If she needed a confirmation that Roald was not stupid, this was it. Not only had he learned the eastern trader's name, he had listened to how it was pronounced. She must find out when and where the two had met.

"Roald, listen." Johanna shuffled closer to him. "You know that day when Alexandre still ruled and we led the procession to the markets where people were going to be burned at the stake, and where we raised all our wooden rakes and shovel handles and they grew into a tree that captured Alexandre and locked him in? And when the nobles who had supported him fled but their ship caught fire and they had to swim to safety?"

He gave her a blank look.

"Well, those nobles survived and some of them are still

around." Although quite a few had left the city. "They're claiming that Li Han burned their ship with magic, and they're claiming that he has fire dragons and that they live inside the belly of his ship—"

"I already told them that it's a machine that works on the pressure of steam locked in a vat."

"I know you did." He had told, too, a big group of people who had been waiting in the palace forecourt back before they got the soup kitchens going. Those people were all homeless and hungry and had merely stared at him. They didn't care. They didn't believe a word he said.

"See? I did tell them." He nodded. For him, the matter of belief did not come into the question. Things were or they were not.

"Those nobles who survived don't like Li Han's presence in the city," she continued.

"But he can teach us a lot."

"Yes, he can, and that's why it's important that people like Johan Delacoeur don't get to control what goes on in the city. He was made *regent*, Roald, and I will certainly not be able to perform any duties for a while. You must come to our meetings, so that you can continue our quest to be a truly independent country. Father will help you."

He looked confused. "You can't preform your duties? What is wrong with you?"

"I'm having a child, the heir to the throne." She cringed while saying that. She couldn't bring herself to saying *your child*, while she very much doubted that the child was Roald's.

A frown. "You look healthy enough to me. Why can't you keep going to the meetings?"

"Because I'm with child. It's not appropriate." And she cringed saying that, too, because it went against everything she had stood for in her life. "The nobles will say that it's not appropriate for the queen to perform duties while she is with child. Roald, I'm not going to have any arguments against them and I'm not going to be able to hide it for much longer. You must come to the meetings. You must show them who is the king."

He stared at her. "I don't like meetings, and those men don't like me."

Johanna spread her hands in frustration. "This is not about liking you. If you're not there when I can't be present, they'll decide things that you like even less. These meetings are very important for the future of Saardam. I want to write to every country and company that uses our seaport to ask if they want to invest in rebuilding the harbour. We need the money, and if all those countries have invested, they won't attack us anymore and risk their projects."

He blinked at her. "That's a good idea. You should do that."

"But I need your help!"

"Those men won't listen to me."

"You're the king! You can tell them what to do."

He gave her a blank look.

"Roald, I need you to come to the council and tell them that you think my idea is good and that they should listen to me."

But as she already knew, it was pointless getting angry at him about not doing his duties. He just did not understand. King Nicholaos and Queen Cygna had bypassed him and appointed his younger sister as successor to the throne. Every day, Johanna was reminded of how sensible a decision that had been. Roald was present in person, but he was never really responsive to what went on around him, unless it concerned beetles or frogs, or, heaven forbid, Rinius.

She stared at the exquisite drawing he had made. He would have made an excellent monk or a student of the natural arts. He would have been good at many things, but not at being a king.

"Let's go to sleep."

"Yes." Roald gathered his paper and brushes and dumped them in the box. "I want to look at you tonight."

Johanna cringed.

He hadn't asked for a while, and she had been quiet about it. Being prodded in sensitive places was honestly something she could do without right now. It made her belly tense up. Sometimes it hurt. Yet she didn't dare say no.

Johanna undressed, first her poor old ripped overdress. She placed it on the chair with a feeling of melancholy, doubting that Nellie would be able to fix the damage. Then she pulled her underdress over her head. She watched herself in the dressing mirror as a pale form in the darkness. Her stomach was very obviously swollen, and anyone who saw her would have no doubt about her condition. She ran her hand over the firm bump and lifted her heavy breasts. They, too, felt very solid and tender.

Roald came to stand behind her, reaching for her belly from behind. His hands were always cold.

"You can feel the child move," she said. She placed his hand on her skin.

They stood like that for a while. Roald's beard tickled her shoulder.

Then he called out, "Yes!" He laughed. "I can feel it!"

He pulled her to the bed, where she took off his coat and his shirt and undershirt. He was not half as pale as she was, which didn't surprise her, given that he spent so much time in the sun in the reed beds with his sleeves and trousers rolled up. He was still very thin and his chest hairless.

She undid his belt and pulled off his trousers while he lay on his back.

They went through the usual routine. She sat on top and

impaled herself on him. It was very sensitive, and to be honest, not very pleasant. He was bumping and tossing her around and she tried to keep in a position where his thrusts inside her would not hit any painful spots, never mind finding pleasure herself. That hadn't happened for a long time, and trying to explain to him what she wanted was a waste of time.

The whole thing was made less pleasant because for some reason he'd started taking much longer to reach his release.

Johanna worried about that. At the quayside, she sometimes heard the crude jokes men made about the prowess—or lack of it—of the powerful noblemen. The inability of older men to "do the job" was apparently a given.

Had that already started?

Was it something she had done or that she had allowed him to eat? Did it mean that he would never father a child?

Afterwards, when Roald had gone to sleep, Johanna lay awake, staring towards the ceiling hidden by darkness. As usual at this time of the day, the child cavorted around inside her belly. It was growing. She dreaded what the king's council would say when she turned up for a meeting when her condition was obvious.

They'd be offended. They'd tell her that they couldn't possibly have a meeting like this.

Johan Delacoeur would rule, and her idea to get the surrounding countries to invest in the harbour would never happen.

He'd tell Li Han that he couldn't have the office.

The Baron would continue to try to get his hands on the city.

Or the Belaman Church.

Li Han would leave, and Johanna would never set foot aboard the iron ship. Li Fai would leave, too, and take his ships to Anglia.

CHAPTER 6

IT WAS NOT a good morning. Johanna woke up feeling ill and things did not get better from there.

She had been told that the sickness only happened at the time that one could not yet tell that a woman was with child, but her body clearly had different ideas.

The tea she'd had for breakfast made a reappearance, and then she was hungry and ate some bread, but that didn't go down too well either.

Feeling listless and ill, she retired to the couch in the living room where Father came to keep her company.

As usual, he had needed to think about an idea before he formed an opinion on it, but his opinion had formed in favour of Johanna's plan. In fact, he'd already drafted a letter to be sent to each of the royal houses in the area, and he had come to show it to her.

He had plans, too. "King Leopold of Burovia has a lot of money and is not averse to trying new things as long as we can show clearly what his benefit will be, so I will draw up a table of returns on investment based on estimates of warehouse hire and mooring fees. I expect to be able to give a positive return after about five years. And that isn't counting any tariffs and trade levies of goods sold. We might even get this grumpypot of a Baron Uti to invest in the seaport because, without it, he'll have to import through Lurezia and he's not a friend of the Lurezian court. I very much doubt that, given the choice, he wants to fight over access to Saardam. Most wise rulers try to limit the number of wars they get involved in. Say what you want about Baron Uti, but he's not dumb."

It was worth trying to get him to invest, Johanna thought, although fighting seemed very much in Baron Uti's arsenal. If King Leopold would commit to making an investment, that would forge a bond between him and the Carmine House. In turn, Baron Uti would not attack something that his cousin King Leopold was involved in.

Father said, "The support of Estland is pretty much a given because of strong ties between the royal houses, and I don't think Lurezia would hesitate to invest either. They are not averse to trying new things, especially if they don't have to send people."

Ultimately, all of the landlocked countries in the east depended on imported goods coming in through Saardam.

Trying to make an attractive proposition to the foreign companies and countries that hoped to sell through the port was a bit trickier. Phoenicia and Anglia could easily go elsewhere, so it was all about premium customers for their produce, about quick unloading and fair quay tariffs.

Father understood what made the captains happy. He proposed preferential unloading treatment and warehouse space in return for the investment.

"For example, Anglia and Phoenicia could each own a warehouse. They would pay for rebuilding that warehouse and in return they would never have to pay storage fees."

That was a scary prospect. Storage fees had always an important source of income for the city.

The idea of foreign countries owning buildings in Saardam was both exhilarating and scary. The name Anglia struck fear in the hearts of many Saarlanders. In the past, conflicts on land had been fought with places in the east. Baron Uti usually had something to do with it. The conflicts at sea were usually fought with King William of Anglia, who had been in power for longer than Johanna had been alive. He had a vastly superior seafaring fleet and was in the process of mapping out all the unknown lands.

If Li Fai made his office in Saardam, and if he was tied to Saardam because he owned the warehouse, the people of the city would eventually have iron ships. If Li Fai was driven out of Saardam by ignorant men "because he had dragon magic," then he might well go to Anglia and would ply his dragon magic there. If that happened, King William might well be the next ruler trying to overthrow the weak royal family of Saardam with the help of eastern magic.

Johanna and Father agreed on many things, and neither of them needed to mention the looming uncertainty hanging over this plan: without Roald's support or understanding, how were they going to get this plan past the King's Council?

While Johanna and Father sat talking, the palace guard she had sent to check the *Lady Sara* came in.

"We can't see much damage to your ship, Your Majesty," he said. "The intruder had a torch but most likely he used it for light."

"Was anything stolen?"

"Not that we can tell. Most valuable items were removed from the hold when the ship first returned." Carpenters had removed the temporary stairs and the old furniture that made up the makeshift room where Johanna and Roald had lived when the ship had lain moored at the riverbank in Florisheim. The *Lady Sara* had gone back from being a houseboat to a river sloop.

She asked, "Was the intruder perhaps a pauper, looking for a dry place to sleep?"

"We can only guess until we can question the man."

And that required knowing who he was and where he was.

Father said, "Look, if there is no damage to the ship, it's not worth worrying about. For all we know, it was a sailor looking at the sky longing for his sweetheart in some faraway town and then getting nervous when he was disturbed in a place he shouldn't have been."

Johanna's sickness subsided after some sweet cakes and tea. Father said he was going to see the mayor to talk about their plan. Apart from Master Deim, he was the person most likely to support it.

Johanna went in search of Roald.

She found Nellie instead, setting the table for the midday meal.

"Whatever did you do to your brown dress, Mistress Johanna?"

"It split while I was at church." That seemed such a long time ago and seemed such a trivial thing to worry about.

"I told you that it was too tight. It is getting really scandalous. I hope you don't mind, but I've asked the modiste to come. She will be here this afternoon. I apologise for the very short notice, but I've waited long enough. I will not have the dresses fall off you while you're in town."

Johanna sighed and let her shoulders slump. Nellie was right, of course.

"Do go and see her," Nellie said, her voice stern.

Johanna nodded.

She went to the room she used as her office, sat down and with a heavy heart wrote an announcement for the town crier.

To the citizens of Saarland: King Roald and Queen Johanna Carmine de Lacoeur van Leeuwen Brouwer announce the impending birth of the first heir to the throne, expected at the end of August. The Queen intends to keep fulfilling her duties to the people of Saardam.

There.

She debated adding *for as long as possible*, but that would be dishonest. She had no intention of giving up her position, ever.

She cringed when she rolled up the parchment and sealed the paper. There was no avoiding it.

Once the modiste came in, the news would spread like wildfire anyway. There was a King's Council meeting tomorrow. It was best that she announce the news rather than that the men hear it in some other way.

Johanna gave the roll of parchment to the guard station in the foyer and went to the dining room.

Roald had come in for the midday meal. He sat at his usual spot at the head of the table. His cheeks were red from sunburn and his jacket was probably still in the garden.

Johanna sat opposite him. "Did you see anything special in the garden today?"

"Lots of frog eggs. There are so many frogs! They're very hard to catch."

But clearly that hadn't stopped him trying. "You have duckweed in your hair."

"Oh?" He ruffled his hair, making it more dishevelled than it already was. The duckweed fell onto his plate. He blew it onto the white tablecloth while the maid came to ladle soup into the plates.

"I want to get ducks for the garden. They eat grass so the gardener won't have to cut the grass anymore."

"But they poo everywhere."

"That's good for the grass. I want to have chickens, too, and I have to grow carrots. They are good for your skin."

Johanna had intended to raise the subject of the foreign investment with him once again. He would have to sign any plan that she and Father made, and she wanted him to understand. He'd said he liked the idea. Why couldn't he just sign the document and let her do whatever needed to be done? But sadly, that was not how Roald worked. Once he got an idea into his head, he was unlikely to listen to anything else.

And frankly, his enthusiasm for the garden was infectious.

A vegetable garden would be nice, Johanna agreed. The queen's rose garden had always struck her as frivolous. Roald could grow carrots, and at harvest, she'd ask the cook to make a lot of carrot and potato soup and hand it out to the poorest citizens. He could grow cabbages, too and they could make cabbage pots and hand those out to poor people in winter.

Roald said he knew exactly how to make cabbage pots, how much vinegar and how much water to use. She suspected he had learned this at the Guentherite farm.

As usual, talking to Roald never failed to take her mind off problems.

Sitting here, with the sunlight streaming in through the window, with a view into the garden that was bright green from spring growth, it was easy to forget how precarious the Carmine House's position was.

It was such a nice day that Johanna followed Roald into the garden after the meal. He chatted endlessly about where he wanted to keep the ducks and the chickens, and where he wanted the carrot bed.

"And we can grow beans over there. No parsnips. I don't like parsnips. I'm the king. If I don't like parsnips, I can just not grow them."

Johanna eyed the empty middle of the old garden. "What shall we do with the fountain?"

When the bandits had removed the statue of the Triune that used to stand on a pedestal in the middle of the pond, they had broken the basin. The water was all gone, and the bottom was covered in dead leaves. Weeds grew in the cracks.

"We can fix it. We can keep fish, and the ducks will have somewhere to swim!"

"What about the statue?"

He frowned.

"The statue of the Triune that used to sit in the middle."

"The church can keep it."

"We can have a new one made."

"No. I don't like the faces on those heads."

The shepherd at church often asked her when the king would come to the evening service. After all, King Nicholaos used to come every day. Johanna usually made a vague reply. In truth she didn't know what Roald thought of his father's obsession with the church. She had tried to keep him away from the subject and never asked him to come. If Rinius was his hero, he would not care for the church. Rinius cared little for religion, and had paid a heavy price for expressing those views openly. Roald could get into a lot of trouble.

It was with a heavy heart that Johanna watched Nellie coming into the garden to announce that the modiste had arrived and was waiting in the Red Room. Back to playing games.

Mistress Daphne had left town or had been killed—no one was sure which. Apparently the modiste where the royal family bought their clothing, even before the fires, was Mistress Dina.

She sat in the Red Room, where the servants had put the two makeshift thrones against the back wall, removed the chairs for the King's Council and replaced those with the couches that normally stood in this room when there was no meeting.

Mistress Dina sat on one of the couches, her basket on the floor next to her. She came from Saardam—no exotic accents this time—and she was a good bit older than Mistress Daphne had been, with her grey hair tied back from her head in a bun.

She rose when Johanna entered and dipped into a curtsy. "You Majesty. I'm your humble servant."

"Good afternoon, Mistress Dina. Do sit down." Oh, how she hated it when people simpered.

Mistress Dina sat, one hand on each knee in perfect symmetry. She looked up at Johanna like a dog waiting for her to throw a stick.

"I seem to be in need of some dresses." Johanna dropped the cape revealing the house dress that she wore underneath, a plain garment that had no laced bodice or anything that hid the rounding in her stomach.

Mistress Dina's eyes widened. "Oh. Your Majesty. Congratulations!"

"Thank you. Unfortunately, I have a problem. None of my current dresses fit me anymore."

"I understand. I will be most happy to help you. When will we have an heir to the throne?"

"At the end of August."

"That is so soon already."

"I have nothing decent to wear when I go out, so I will need something quickly."

"You're lucky. There have been many women in your situation. I might have just the thing."

Mistress Dina put her basket on the couch and started taking items out. Johanna thought back to the time that Mistress Daphne had come with her giant boxes that contained hideously frilled evening dresses. For some reason, she wanted something bold and colourful and outrageous like Mistress Daphne would propose.

But the samples that Mistress Dina put on the couch were all dark-coloured, heavy material. And then she dug up a larger bundle of material. "I have one dress here that I can adapt quickly so that you can have something to wear while I make the other ones."

She helped Johanna out of her housedress. The servants had been so thoughtful to carry the mirror from the bedroom. Johanna glanced at herself in her underdress. The bulge in her stomach was really very obvious. She put her hand on the top of its firm roundness.

"Look at you," Mistress Dina said. "When Nellie called me, I had a suspicion, but you certainly have been clever in hiding it this long." She helped Johanna into the dress she had brought. Is was dark grey and made from heavy fabric.

The sleeves came all the way down to her wrists and the bodice buttoned up right up to her chin. Instead of at the waist, the skirt went all the way up to just under her breasts.

She looked at herself in the mirror. The fabric was so heavy and thick that the folds hid the curve in her stomach. Johanna pulled the fabric around her so that it drew taut around her front.

"Yes, the dress hides it very discretely."

Yet it was very obviously a type of dress that would only be worn by a woman with child. Johanna wasn't sure that now she announced it officially, she wanted to hide it discretely. She'd want Mistress Daphne to design something outrageous in bright pink with a huge frilly bow, or something ridiculous.

"It's going to be summer. I'll be so hot in this dress," Johanna protested.

"Well, you can't wear any of those Lurezian flimsy gowns. Imagine, in some of those, people can see right in between here." She held her hand over her bosom. "You are already quite heavy in the bosom. You do not want men staring at the rounding of your bust or your stomach. You want a dress that covers all the indecent bits. It's not meant to be flattering.

Mind you, you will have no waist so being flattering is nigh impossible."

No, indeed. Johanna stared at herself in the mirror, dismayed at the dreadful dress. Was *this* what she was going to have to wear for the next few months?

Mistress Dina made her stand with her arms wide while she measured and scribbled on her slate. Then, with all the measurements taken, she told Johanna to keep the dress on.

"It's a bit wide in the shoulders. I will fix it later, but it's almost church time and you can't possibly turn up to church in your house dress."

Johanna looked wistfully at the dress draped over the back of the couch and again at herself in the mirror. The dress was a horrible, shapeless thing. She looked as if she were going to a funeral. Even her dark red cape was going to be outrageously colourful compared to this thing.

She looked like . . .

Like the old women who sat in the back of the church.

And then Johanna realised that this was a setup. Mistress Dina was sent by the shepherd or someone like that. Get her to dress properly in church-approved clothes.

Because no one in the church thought that her clothes were dour enough.

Hot anger made her cheeks flush.

The church was trying to make her and Roald theirs, as they had done with King Nicholaos.

CHAPTER 7

HAD SHE BEEN plain Johanna Brouwer, she would probably have stopped going to church at that point. She had only started going to church a few years before the fires, because so many people spoke about it, and because the services were very well attended and the wooden pews told her many stories about the people who sat in them.

But she had left Johanna Brouwer behind ages ago, and more than ever, she realised that her survival, indeed the survival of Saarland as independent country, relied on a careful balance between the Church of the Triune and the Belaman Church, between magic and those who abhorred it, between true Saarlanders and those from elsewhere.

Had she been plain Johanna Brouwer, she might have barged into the service late wearing her clogs, stormed to the altar and yelled at the shepherd at the top of her voice for trying to make her do what he wanted. She'd have dressed in the most colourful dress, too.

But she'd been young and naïve and if it weren't for Father

she would probably have ended up at the bottom of the Saar River.

So she wore the dour dress, but even Father noticed it. He frowned. "Is that your new dress? It's not like you at all."

Johanna mumbled something about being proper.

"Dear child, when have you ever worried about something being proper?" Master Deim was just coming in. He eyed Johanna's dress. "Yes, that's very . . . unlike you."

Johanna made a lame excuse. "Mistress Dina came with Nellie's recommendation. She's been modiste for the royal family for years."

"Hmm. Very motherly." That dress had to be bad if even Father noticed it.

Not so long ago, she had worn clogs to church. How quickly things changed.

Father nodded his approval. "Well, at least no one at the King's Council will be speculating anymore."

"Did they speculate?" Not that it should surprise her.

"There was some rather crude talk, which I put an end to. Tomorrow's meeting will be interesting if you are going to be stubborn about being on the council."

Interesting was not the word Johanna would use. One thing she appreciated about Father. No matter how much he, as a man, would disagree with her desire to continue working, he had never said anything about it.

Fortunately, the day had turned quite cold, and Johanna could wear her cape over the top without dying of heat stroke. She was glad of the comfort the coach offered her on the way to church.

A group of citizens waited on the steps and under porch, sheltering against the steady drizzle that had started to fall. As soon as the driver opened the coach door, a cheer went up.

A man shouted over the top of all the voices, "Three cheers for the queen and the royal heir!"

People shouted, "Hurray, hurray, hurray!" And then they clapped and shouted "Congratulations!"

In her new and very dour "proper" dress, Johanna felt like a dressed-up doll. No, she was a puppet like those in the puppet theatre. Someone else did the talking. She just did whatever people expected. Her body was reduced to being a vessel to carry the royal heir.

It's your own fault, a little voice inside her said. *No one ever said that it would be easy.* As sole heiress of the Brouwer Company, her life was always a commodity anyway. To be married off. Sleep with this man and beget him an heir. That was her function.

A very, very small corner in her mind found it funny that the child that would be born in August carried no Carmine blood and would probably have a good deal of magic.

Inside the church it smelled of wet fabric and musty clothes. Most people would have walked here through the rain. Most people who came to church were the merchants and workers. Very few nobles would ever have set foot inside this building or even its predecessor, or, for that matter, any of the other Church of the Triune buildings in town.

Johanna sat down at the usual pew at the very front of the church. She could still feel people's gazes and hear people talking about her and the impending birth. Most of the talk was good, happy. Nellie had been right.

Then someone behind her said in a clear voice, "What is *he* doing here?"

And someone else gasped.

Johanna glanced at the guard next to her. He had half-risen from the pew and looked out towards the back of the church.

"Who are they talking about?" she asked him in a

low voice.

"Have a look yourself. You wouldn't believe me if I told you."

She looked over her shoulder.

At the very back of the church there was an area for late-comers. There were always people who came after the service had started and couldn't get a seat, and a few people always preferred to stand. They were usually the same people: a farmer who lived just outside the town and who complained that sitting hurt his backside, a quay hand who was so tall that his legs didn't fit comfortably between the rows of pews.

Today, someone else had joined them: a man in a thick fur coat with black hair tied back in a bun. Li Fai.

Whether it was coincidence or a work of magic, he found Johanna's eyes over the heads of all those people.

She felt like screaming at him, *Leave! This is not a place that's friendly to you!* She wondered what had possessed him to come here. If he was naively curious about what people did at church, this curiosity would kill him one day. If he had a plan . . . what plan could possibly involve a church that preached against his very existence?

If she were plain Johanna Brouwer, she would have gone to him right now and asked him if he knew what he was doing. But if she were plain Johanna Brouwer, she would probably hardly know who he was. Or she would, like most people, be afraid that he was an evil magician.

Even if she entertained that thought to get up and warn him anyway, it was too late for it now, because the congregation hushed and the shepherd came to the dais. He wore his usual cream-coloured robe and a red scarf that hung down both sides of his neck. The sign of the Triune—two triangles with the sides intertwined—was embroidered in gold thread on both ends of the scarf and the tassels dangled as he walked.

He met Johanna's eyes and bowed. Then he opened the big, leatherbound *Book of Verses* that lay on the dais and started the service. Today, he spoke about the good of the holy god and how that good lived on in each person.

He seemed . . . distracted, for want of a better word. He was constantly leafing through the book looking for specific citations. Twice he forgot where he was. Johanna noticed that he looked thin, and his hands trembled. Several times, he glanced at the back of the church where Li Fai stood. Johanna was afraid that he was going to make comments about "heathen invaders", but he did not.

After the service, he came down the steps and bowed to Johanna. "You have formally announced the impending birth. My congratulations."

"How is Greetje?" His wife had to be very close to giving birth.

"Very well."

"She must be getting very tired. I have hardly seen her in the past month."

"She has been busy." He glanced aside. "All of her work has been in the house. It's not a good idea for a woman in her condition to go about in the streets."

Johanna wanted to argue why not, and that women on farms didn't seem to have those restrictions, but other women had already assured her that she'd be too tired to do anything that wasn't essential, and her first consideration should be for the child. Never having had a child, Johanna couldn't dispute their statements. What did she know about it anyway?

She wanted to talk to Li Fai, so she made some sort of an excuse and went down the aisle towards the back of the church. But there were so many people wanting to congratulate her that by the time she came to the area behind the pews, Li Fai was nowhere to be seen.

The church buzzed with rumour about him, but so many women crowded around to offer Johanna help and advice that she couldn't hear what was being said. The women offered to make clothes and bedding for the little one. They offered to help look after the child, wet-nursing even.

It made Johanna feel uneasy. This was actually getting serious. It was happening. This annoying thing that grew inside her would always be part of her life. There was no going back.

That was a scary thought.

She looked over her shoulder, but the shepherd was gone, too. That was strange. He normally never let an opportunity pass to talk to the congregation.

Johanna put the facts together.

Li Fai coming to church, now gone. The shepherd nervous, now also gone.

"Let's go," she said to her guard, who today was Anton, a soft-spoken orange-haired giant. With his imposing figure, he had no trouble clearing the aisle and preceded her to the doors.

"Wait," Johanna said when she was in the coach and he was about to shut the door. "I'd like you to walk around the church, especially the back of the building where few people go except the shepherd."

"Anything in particular you want me to look for, Your Majesty?"

"Anything unusual, but in particular people having arguments."

He nodded without question and vanished into the night.

Johanna waited in the coach while the last of the congregation filed out of the church. It was very dark in the porch of the church, and a few pitiful street lamps reflected in the wet wooden steps.

Up on the driver's seat, the coach driver sneezed so loudly

that it echoed over the market square. His movement made the coach wobble a little. One of the horses snorted, probably having been suddenly awoken from its nap.

Johanna giggled silently. She had no idea why she found it funny when people sneezed.

But now there was a sound of a key being turned in a lock. A moment later a figure in a rain cloak walked across the porch and down the steps. This person was too small to either be the shepherd. It had to be one of the altar boys.

Johanna opened the door to the coach. "Excuse me."

The boy—because it was indeed an altar boy—gasped audibly. "Oh. Your Majesty. I didn't realise you were still here."

Johanna managed to stop herself from saying *The coach would have been a pretty good indication.* "I was wondering if there is something going on with the shepherd. Normally he closes the church, doesn't he?"

"Yes, he does. He asked me to close tonight."

"Did he say why?"

"He didn't, Your Majesty."

"Is it because of his wife?"

"I honestly couldn't tell, Your Majesty. Could be."

That was typical of Master Willems: he rarely spoke about his family or anything that could be considered personal information.

While they stood there, Anton came around the corner of the church building. He shook his head. "Nothing. All quiet."

Johanna sighed. Maybe she was seeing things. "Let's go home then."

"As you wish."

Johanna went back into the cabin, and Anton climbed on the bench next to the driver. The coach set off.

The rain had gotten heavier in the past few minutes. Drops streaked over the little window and restricted Johanna's view of the deserted streets. The coach went the long way. In the past few days, the town council had started repaving the main street from the markets to the palace, and with the rain it would be muddy. So they went along the stately houses along the main canal and turned left into the street that ran from the markets to the harbour.

They were almost at the markets when Johanna became aware of voices: men shouting. The coach slowed down and then stopped.

Anton said, "All in order?"

A man replied. Johanna couldn't hear what he said. She opened the door to the coach far enough that she could stand on the top step and look into the street. Cold rain hit her face.

Five men stood in a circle. Four wore dark clothing and hoods that covered their heads. One of those carried a torch.

The fifth man, with his back against the steps to the front door of a stately house, was Li Fai.

He met Johanna's eyes over the rump of one of the horses. An expression of relief came to his eyes.

Johanna couldn't see who the other men were, but one wore a long coat of thick felt or some such. It was a fine-looking garment that a pauper could never afford. The other men weren't paupers either.

"Do ride with us." She put on her most innocent voice. "The weather is positively awful. We can go past your ship. I wanted to ask some questions, if you don't mind being questioned at this time of day."

He bowed. "I'm at your service." In long strides, he walked past the four men to the coach. As he passed, one of them turned his head, allowing a brief flash of torchlight to strike his face.

It was Octavio Nieland.

CHAPTER 8

L I FAI CLIMBED into the cabin and sat down on the bench opposite Johanna. Anton shut the door behind him, enveloping Johanna in the smell of wet clothing and the faint tag of a foreign perfume.

The coach jolted into motion.

"Thank you," Li Fai said, pressing his hands together before his chest and bowing.

There was a short silence, thick and awkward.

"Were they bothering you?"

"They were asking things I don't know."

"Do you know any of these men? Have you met them before?"

"They have businesses in the harbour, don't they? One is from the Nieland family?"

Johanna nodded. "What did they want to know? They didn't hurt you, did they?" It was far too dark in the coach to see if he had any injuries to his face.

"No." He let a short silence lapse, in which Johanna filled in, *Not yet*, and then continued. "A few months before we came here, we put in at Seneza. We come there often."

Johanna had heard sailors talk about Seneza. She didn't think Father had ever been there. Lurezia was about the furthest south one could travel on the inland rivers. Seneza lay at a rocky point where the Golden Sea joined the southern Lamorian Ocean. From accounts, she had heard it was a sunny and dry place, with a jumble of ochre-painted houses and many ancient temples and churches. It had been the home of the Belaman Church for hundreds of years, and it was because of its location that the church had so easily spread across the known lands.

Seneza was also an important port city, which was why Li Han would have been there, going in and out of the Golden Sea to Phoenicia and many of the rich lands in that area.

"While we were in Seneza, something important was happening there, except we were unfamiliar with it at the time. Apparently there was an inquisition in the Belaman Church."

Johanna nodded. The one where the Most Holy Father Severino had declared the Church of the Triune banned from the Belaman Church.

"On the evening before our departure, a man came to us. He asked if we were going to Saardam, and we said we were. Then he asked us if we could take a crate and deliver it to the shepherd of the Church of the Triune. We said we could. He paid the fee. We did as asked."

"Was that why you were in the church tonight?"

"No. We delivered the crate when we first moored at the quay weeks ago. But people have been asking about it since. I was . . . simply curious about the church and trying to understand why so many people are looking for this thing. I was going to ask the shepherd what was in the crate."

"You didn't look at it while it was on your ship?"

"We trust our customers and do not open their cargo." He sounded indignant.

"I'm sorry. I just thought you might have had to inspect the contents or something. Did you end up asking the shepherd what was inside?"

"He left the church before I could go to him. It was very busy."

Indeed, it had been, but also, having seen Li Fai, the shepherd had left the church quickly. "And these men who were just talking to you, they asked about this thing as well?"

"They did."

This was getting ever stranger. "What did they want to know?"

"They asked me where it is, not believing me when I said we delivered it to the shepherd. They say the shepherd tells them he doesn't have it. So if he doesn't have it, what did he do with it? Why should that be our business? We delivered it. Our business is finished." He spread his hands. "But still they come. They believe the shepherd, and not our words. We don't have anything to do with it. We don't have it anymore."

"Who gave it to you, in Seneza?"

"It was a man from the church. He paid us on the spot and didn't want his name recorded. That is not unusual. Some people are very suspicious. He was quite old and was wearing . . ." He made a movement down his front indicating a long garment. "He was a monk."

"A habit?"

"Yes."

Very strange indeed. "Have any of these people told you why they want it?"

"They seem to think it is worth more than the gold we brought."

The coach was turning onto the quay. The wheels rattled over the cobblestones.

She spoke in a low voice. "Did the crate contain something of . . . magic?"

"Magic?" He frowned.

"Yes, like . . ." Her heart was thudding hard against her ribs. "Like if I touch a piece of wood, the wood can tell me what it has seen in the few days before. Some people can see things on the wind, or in water." She didn't know why she was saying this. He was still frowning and clearly had no idea what she was talking about.

From the brief encounter in the palace, she *thought* he had magic, but maybe he didn't. Maybe there was no magic in his homeland.

Still, she continued, speaking even more quietly now. "Some people can make trees grow very quickly. So quickly that they can trap their enemies inside."

His eyes widened. "The tree in the market square. The one with the ugly speckled leaves." His voice was no more than a whisper. "It cries."

Johanna nodded, and she knew for certain. Only people with magic could hear the cry of Alexandre's angry soul. "This is what I mean. Some people can make trees do their will. Other people can shape fire into creatures."

"You call that magic?"

"Yes. What do you call it?"

"Art." He drew something from his pocket and held it in the palm of his hand: a finely made octagonal wooden box. A faint orange glow emanated from a dragon pattern of inlaid wood and mother-of-pearl on the lid.

Johanna held her breath.

"Touch it," he said.

She reached out and brushed the very tips of her fingers over the wood. She saw the inside of a ship's cabin. A couple of lamps hung from the ceiling. Li Han sat by the window. On his lap he held a bundle of cloth that looked like a jacket or robe and he was pulling a needle with bright red thread through the fabric. On the back of the jacket he had embroidered the top half of a dragon in exquisite detail.

Li Fai's mother Wen Mei sat at a desk surrounded by jars of paint and brushes. She was painting on silk cloth held in a wooden frame. Johanna recognised the flowers she was drawing: a daisy, a dandelion, buttercups, cornflowers, poppies. Behind her on a low shelf against the wall stood a number of finished drawings, of ducks, rabbits, deer, cows, and one with a couple of green frogs.

"Do you see what the wood says?" Li Fai asked.

"Yes. I see your parents. Your mother is drawing plants and creatures from our land. Your father is doing embroidery."

He nodded. "The box contains my art." The glow of the dragon pattern on the lid had intensified.

He opened the lid and some brightly glowing thing came out.

Johanna gasped and withdrew her hand.

The thing cavorted through the air between them, trailing sparks in its wake. Eventually it settled in the palm of Li Fai's hand. It was . . . a miniature dragon. It crouched like a dog waiting for its master to throw a stick, swishing its tail. Its eyes were buggy like a frog's, and roved from Li Fai to her and back.

Li Fai said something and it jumped into the air before running over his arm, across his shoulder, behind his head, over the other shoulder and down his other arm. Then it jumped onto Johanna's knee. She gave a squeak and shrank back. It ran over the seat before jumping onto the ledge under the window in the coach door and jumped from there onto her shoulder, and used that as a springboard to jump to Li Fai's hand, where it sat back on its haunches, waiting for the next command.

"What is it?" Johanna asked. She ran her hand over her knee, checking the dress for fire damage, but found none.

"This is my art. This is my dragon. It does what I say." He again gave it a command, and it jumped from his hand to Johanna's knee and crouched there, looking at her like a little puppy.

"It's cute."

"You can touch it."

She carefully reached out and touched the creature's back. It was smooth and firm. "It's warm." The flames that trailed off the flanks and the comb-like plates over the creature's spine weren't hot, as she expected.

"That's because it's a dragon." That clearly explained everything.

"I'm not familiar with dragons."

It yawned widely, and then dropped onto its belly, resting its head onto its forepaws.

"It likes you."

Johanna chuckled. "Where did you get this creature?"

"You don't 'get' dragons. When a child with the art is born, the child's grandfather goes to the dragon temple and receives a box. The child is then schooled to fill it with whatever art he or she excels at."

"So . . . if I grew up in your lands, my box would have. . . ?"

"A small tree."

Johanna tried to imagine what that would look like. She imagined opening the box and a little tree would gently unfold from inside. The branches would be supple and thin, waving as if moved by an unseen breeze. That breeze, of course, would contain stories other people could read. The tree drank the water that told yet others their stories. In that moment, she understood the power of wood magic and knew that she had never understood it before.

Her voice was soft when she said, "Could you show me how to make a tree grow in a box?"

He shook his head, his expression sad. "I don't know if I can. I can try, but it is something for a child to learn. I haven't taught children."

"Do you have any children?"

"I have not yet been married."

Which wasn't the same thing at all, but it seemed rude to point out the difference.

She was vaguely aware that the coach had stopped. Li Fai snapped his fingers. The dragon jumped up into the wooden box, leaving a warm spot on Johanna's knee. Li Fai shut the lid. The mosaic dragon on the lid glowed for a second or two before fading.

There were footsteps outside, followed by Anton opening the door. "We're at the gentleman's ship, Your Majesty."

A blast of cold air came into the cabin.

Li Fai put the box into his pocket. He bowed to Johanna, meeting her eyes. "It was an honour to be given a ride with you."

"It was my pleasure."

He rose and hesitated at the top of the steps. He said in a low voice, "The crate we carried for the shepherd was art. Even when I wasn't in the hold, I could feel the chill of it. My father was upset with me when I said we should throw it overboard. He agreed to take it and he got the monk's money. My father does not have art. He doesn't understand. I said I wouldn't have taken it, because the art is not a good kind. There was much death in the crate. If it is lost, do not look for it. It is a bad thing."

He bowed again and then he was gone, leaving behind a cold silence that didn't dissipate even after Anton had shut the door.

CHAPTER 9

JOHANNA STARED OUT the little window while the coach made its way back to the palace. She felt dumb and ignorant. There were places out there where magic was taught routinely to children. Why did she have to be born in a place where it was swept under the carpet, denied and even forbidden?

She imagined Father going up to a building called a "dragon temple" and coming back with a box for her to contain and focus her magic. Her life would have been . . . so much happier. Instead, she'd been angry, she'd bumbled through dealing with magic and trying to hide it. She'd thought that by going to a church that forbade magic she could change people's opinions of her. Obviously Master Willems still thought that.

What a fool she'd been.

On the driver's seat, Anton and the driver were telling jokes. Their laughter echoed in the empty streets that glistened with the rainwater.

The coach dropped Johanna off at the bottom of the

palace steps. A guard with flickering storm light met her there and accompanied her to the entrance.

Johanna pulled the sides of her cloak together. It always was cold and blustery here. The sea wind whipped up across the wide expanse of the Saar delta on the other side of the palace.

She just came into the foyer when another guard entered from the hallway. His face showed an expression of relief as if he'd been waiting for her. He bowed. "My excuses for the late hour, but you have a visitor, Your Majesty."

Her heart jumped. "Who is this visitor?" Her first thought was *Li Han*, wanting a reply about the office, and she was not in a position to give him that reply yet. There was the King's Council still to be convinced of her plan. Yes, she could override the council and give him permission to find an office along the quayside, but doing so would make her life pretty hard, because many of the men in the King's Council would never cooperate with her again.

"She didn't say her name. I asked her to wait in the Red Room."

"I'll go and see her now."

Her. Not Li Han, obviously. Johanna's next thought, while walking down the hallway, was *Loesie*.

It even made sense. Loesie could feel magic and if this thing that Li Han had taken to the shepherd was something of great magic, Loesie would know about it.

Johanna reached the Red Room. Because there were no meetings tomorrow, no one had bothered to light the fire in the hearth and it was unpleasantly cold in the room. The air smelled of moisture with a faint whiff of mould.

Someone had lit a few oil lights, but they did little to dispel the cloying darkness that hung in this room at the best of times.

On the couch in the middle of the room sat a small

person hiding under a hooded cloak of green velvet. This was definitely not Loesie, because she wore only black.

As Johanna entered and the guard shut the door behind her, a pair of pale, slender hands came out from under the cloak and pushed back the hood.

Greetje, wife of Master Willems, now Shepherd Victor.

But what a sight she was. Her hair hung loose down both sides of her face, her left eye was swollen and a nasty bruise coloured her cheekbone.

Johanna gasped and raised her hand to her mouth. "What happened to you?"

Greetje's chin trembled. Her eyes glittered with tears. Her voice was hoarse, no more than a whisper. "He's gone mad."

"Who?"

"My husband." The tears rolled over her cheeks.

"He did this to you?" Timid, shy Master Willems?

Greetje nodded, choking out a sob. She gingerly wiped her face, wincing as she touched the bruised cheekbone.

"But how is that possible? He is the shepherd." But that of course didn't guarantee his behaviour.

Johanna saw the shepherd as he had made his way out of the church earlier that night. He hadn't even stayed behind after the service to answer questions and talk, as he usually did.

She saw him as she had left him in the church last night: kneeling, praying and chanting, just because she had said the word "necromancer" and hinted that he might want to use his wind magic for the good of Saarland. Because they could do with as many magicians as they could muster. Earlier yesterday, he had argued vehemently against accepting Li Han's money based on a fear of any magic Li Han might have.

She felt cold inside.

"How long has this been going on?"

"He's never hit me before, but he's been acting so

strangely in the last few weeks. It's getting worse."

"Any idea why?"

Greetje shook her head.

"It wouldn't happen to have anything to do with something that he received from the eastern trader?"

She continued shaking her head, although she didn't meet Johanna's eyes. A tear tracked across her cheek. She sniffed. "He's just gone mad."

"Can you tell me what happened? You said he'd been acting strangely, but what does he do that is strange? What does he talk about at the dinner table?"

Greetje laughed, not in an amused way. "He rarely still comes to dinner. When he comes home, he goes upstairs. A room up there used to be a spare bedroom. We were planning to put our little one in there when he or she doesn't need nightly feeds anymore, but he's taken over the room with scary things."

"Like what?"

"The room has dark wallpaper. It used to be his grandfather's smoking room and it still smells of smoke. It has heavy curtains which are always closed. He's put an altar against the wall and filled it up with . . . awful things, like animal skulls and sheep's horns and chicken feet and teeth of things that live in the sea I can't even begin to imagine." She shivered. "There are crudely-made stone statues and puppets made out of straw."

Johanna thought of the primitive altar she had seen when staying in that really poor village on the edge of the shifting sands. She suspected these things were all religious relics.

"When he comes home, he doesn't talk to anyone. He sits on his knees and prays. Often, he cries. He stays in that room for hours on end. His father will ask him to come out, but he never replies. Even if he does come out, he's not really there. He stares into the distance and then he will just snap at someone for no obvious reason at all." Greetje sniffed. "I don't understand. He used to be so nice and gentle. Now, he spends much longer at church and he screams at me when he comes home. He screams at the servants. He doesn't eat. He scares everyone. He sits on his knees in that room all night, praying. Sometimes he cries."

"I really need you to answer this: did he receive anything in a crate recently? Something that was taken to him by the eastern traders and that came from a monk in Seneza?"

Greetje looked at her with wide eyes and shook her head. "Not that I know, but he doesn't tell me anything anymore."

"Then tell me why he hit you."

"I just couldn't bear to listen to his crying and pleading anymore and went into that horrible room. I asked him to please tell us what bothers him so much, so that we can help him, and then he got up and came at me at me." Her mouth trembled. "He took me by the shoulders and pushed me into the wall. He yelled at me that we were all going to die, that the Triune would pass judgment and that we would all end up facing the Lord of Fire because we weren't worthy. I asked him why ever he thought we weren't worthy, because I said he was doing so many good things, and then he started scream-ing. I was really scared because I'd never seen him like that. His eyes were all red and there was spit flying out of his mouth. I didn't even hear any of what he was saying. He looked like a madman. He screamed at me to get out and hit me in the face. Thankfully the groundsman came in. He pulled him away from me, but you should have seen the look in his eyes. As if he could kill me."

She sobbed into her hands, her shoulders shaking with cries. Johanna put her arm on Greetje's shoulders. Goodness, her shoulders were so thin that she could feel the bones through the coat. "I'm sorry for bothering you, but I have nowhere to go. I have no family left."

Master Willems, too, had no family that she could call on for support.

"Of course you can't go back there," Johanna said. "I simply will not have it."

"Please don't call the guards or anyone. He's not himself. I don't know. Something has taken possession of him. Please, he's not a bad man."

"Maybe not, but all the same, you can't go back there in your condition until he calms down. You have the little one to think about."

Greetje looked down and sniffed. "But he will be so angry with me."

"We'll worry about that later. First, we'll give you a safe place to sleep. How long before the little one is born?"

"It could be any day now. I'm so tired."

Johanna called for Nellie and they installed Greetje in the guest room. The maid brought a nightgown which Greetje put on over her round belly. She looked terribly out of proportion, with her arms and legs very thin and her belly hideously swollen. Her navel had even turned inside out and sat like a little bump on a tightly-stretched water bag.

She was exhausted and had evidently been very cold. She was asleep in moments, her cheeks glowing healthy red.

Johanna and Nellie tiptoed out of the room.

"Well, that is a really terrible thing to have happened to her right now," Nellie said. "What are you going to do about the shepherd, Mistress Johanna?"

Johanna sighed. "I don't know. It worries me. The church has so much power over the people. Greetje is right: his words have become so much angrier recently. There is clearly something going on. This is not how it used to be under Shepherd Romulus."

"No, but Shepherd Romulus had it easy. He never knew about the decision by the Belaman Church to expel the

Church of the Triune. He never saw his life's work burned to ashes. The church was new and no one challenged him."

Johanna felt cold. She was going to say, *Don't you start making excuses for him, too, Nellie*, but she wasn't even sure that Nellie would understand. She had come from a church family after all. Was there anyone except the nobles and Father who did not crawl at the shepherd's feet?

Sometimes Johanna thought that ousting Alexandre had been the easiest of their problems.

She said, "Greetje will stay here for a while until we sort out what's going on. Ask the modiste to come and bring us some gowns for a newborn." She held up a finger. "Not Mistress Dina, please."

Nellie gave her a wide-eyed look. "Whatever is wrong with Mistress Dina?"

"Find someone a bit younger who can dress both the child and myself in more cheerful clothing."

"Whatever is wrong with your new dress, Mistress Johanna?"

Johanna spread her arms. "Do I look like a picture of happiness?"

Nellie looked her up and down and frowned. "You look decent to me. Very appropriate."

"I don't want to look decent. I want to look happy. If I have to wear this horrible hot dress, I want you to get me a big silk ribbon to tie around my belly."

Nellie gasped.

"I don't want to look like I'm at a funeral. Find someone, please, who can make me a dress that's comfortable and a bit more cheerful."

Nellie's expression was still bewildered. "I'll do my best. You do know that Mistress Daphne is no longer in town?"

"I do." It was the last thing Johanna had ever expected to be sorry about.

CHAPTER 10

THE RAIN CLEARED overnight for a sunny morning. At breakfast, Roald announced that he was going to start on the vegetable garden. The day was clear, the sky hazy blue and the lawn full of daisies and buttercups. Johanna wished that she could go outside with him, but there was so much still to be done.

The maid confirmed that Greetje was awake and had been brought her breakfast.

Johanna went to see her. In the hallway, she asked a guard. "Has the shepherd been here to visit his wife yet?"

"No, Your Majesty, he hasn't."

That was a bit worrying. Johanna hoped that he was all right. Maybe, if there was time, she should go and see him and ask him about this mysterious crate.

Greetje lay back in the pillows in the bed in the guest room. Sunlight streamed in through the window. A tray with an empty plate and a teapot stood on the table next to the bed. The blanket was pulled up over her belly.

In the daylight the bruises in her face stood out like huge

purple blotches. The eye above the bruise had gone red and bloodshot.

She brought her hand to her face when she noticed Johanna looking at it. "It doesn't hurt so much anymore, but it probably looks terrible."

Johanna nodded. "It's very colourful. How are you feeling, other than that?"

"Tired, but that is probably a permanent thing until I have this child." Her eyes glittered with tears again. "You know, I'd imagined that we'd be a happy family. In the beginning, he told me that he really wanted to be a father, but he lost interest. I don't know what's wrong with him."

"Do you want me to try to talk to him?"

Did Johanna imagine it or did Greetje actually wince at the thought? "I can't imagine that it would do much good."

"But you can't continue like this."

Greetje shrugged.

Well, if the worst came to the worst, she could always let Greetje stay in return for work in the kitchen or laundry. However, the palace was fast filling up with people who were there because she felt sorry for them rather than that they were good at their jobs.

It was not to be helped.

Johanna sent a guard to tell Helena to see Greetje, and went to her office to tackle the urgent correspondence. That pile contained some issues that she should deal with, before the inevitable and probably soon time that the men would no longer let her attend the meetings.

One of those issues was that letter from Joris Decamp, Saardam's mayor, that detailed the pitiful state of the city's stores of grain and potatoes. It was another few months until harvest, and while it was summer, the farming villages had been hit by the fire demons even harder than the city. Crops had gone unplanted because there was simply no one left to do the planting and work the fields. Unless they could get some crops in the ground, the summer would be bad, but the next winter would be devastating.

Another worry was the slow pace of repairs to the city that left many without decent roofs over their heads and forced citizens to walk long distances because canal bridges had been burned.

A few weeks ago, Johanna had asked the city's carpenters, bricklayers and stonemasons how much it would cost to rebuild two key bridges over the main canal.

She had received a stack of quotes, but every single one of them was hideous, as if the city's carpenters had decided en masse that since she was a woman, she couldn't possibly have any idea of how much a new bridge would cost to build. As if she had any of that kind of money to spend.

At least, Li Han's gold would go a long way towards solving those problems in the short term. In the long term, she would just have to convince them to let her write to foreign royal families and merchants to convince them to invest in Saardam's port.

She had the letters all ready. The only thing needed was the approval of a bunch of self-centred men.

After she had sat there staring at her desk and not doing anything, there was a knock on the door and a courtier came in with the news that the King's Council was gathering in the Red Room.

This was it.

Johanna rose from the desk, feeling nervous and sweaty. She checked her reflection in the window: it showed a very proper, very prim young woman with a slight telltale rounding of the stomach. When she pulled the dress flat over her stomach, the bump became more pronounced, and sucking in a breath no longer made it disappear.

Clearly, there was no avoiding the issue.

She picked up her letters and her plan that detailed investment amounts and lists of proposed benefits and went down the corridor to the Red Room.

The men had been talking, but fell quiet when she came in. Johanna crossed the room under their penetrating gazes. She felt like a stock animal for sale.

In total silence, she sat down on the makeshift throne, her pile of papers on her lap. "Well, then, let's begin."

This was followed by an intense silence.

Then Thomas Kloostermans spoke up. "We are of the opinion that you should not be working in your condition." He was a pompous fellow, dressed in an ostentatious white shirt with an abundance of lace on the collar.

"That is a matter for me to decide, isn't it?" She gave him a stern look, but by the Triune, her heart was thudding against her ribs.

"Well . . . Your Majesty. I don't think so. Anything you do will harm the future heir to the throne. The royal family is already in much danger. We cannot risk losing another heir."

"And that apart from the fact that it's simply not appropriate," Patrice Faber said.

"Yes, scandalous," another added.

This statement brought a lot of agreement from the men. Father and Master Deim both watched, their faces blank. The shepherd wasn't there, not that he would have supported her, but that was another thing to worry about.

Johanna picked up the top sheet of her plan. "Gentlemen, why don't we start the meeting. I have many other things to do. I have a proposal that will bring prosperity and lasting peace to Saardam. If you're all quiet, I can read it out—"

Old Patrice Faber said, "What would these foreign visitors think of us, letting a woman work like that. No wonder her decisions have been irrational lately."

Irrational? "Excuse me, I am your queen—" *and you should shut up.*

"Darling, you are the consort. In absence of the king, the King's Council has been instated to make sure that the country stays on the right path until such time that the King's heir—" and he looked pointedly at her stomach "—is old enough to reign in his own name."

"What if it's a girl? What if—" Johanna had to stop herself. She'd almost said it *what if this child is not even Roald's.*

"Dear girl, you will not stop at one child. Where there is one, more will always follow. Your task is to bring a healthy heir into this world."

"My task is to look after the king's affairs because he cannot look after his own."

"That's what *we* are for."

"Roald doesn't want you."

"Then he should turn up to meetings and tell us so. You have been all too quick in speaking on his behalf."

Johanna spread her hands, and let them fall. Every single one of the men, except Father and Master Deim, regarded her with hostility. She met Father's eyes. The expression of defeat on his face hit her hard. He glanced at the door as if he wanted to say, "Just go. It's not to be helped."

Johanna looked around the wall of hostile faces. She found it hard to breathe. She wanted to scream at them that she would bring Roald in and he would tell them that she could keep working just fine. But Roald had never performed on command, and there was no reason why he should do so now.

Thomas Kloostermans gestured at the door.

Unable to find anything to say to counter the demand, Johanna got up.

"Would you like some help?" Master Deim said.

Johanna nodded. She was trembling so much that she feared her legs would give way before she made it to the door.

Master Deim took her arm. Before leaving the room, he said in his gentle voice, "I will represent the Queen's viewpoint. In most cases, it also happens to be my own."

Johanna barely knew how she made her way out of the room.

"It's not fair!" she burst out when they were in the corridor. Hot angry tears pricked in her eyes. In the trek through the forest with the bandits, she had learned some interesting words. She felt very tempted to use them.

"I know, child. But you do have to agree that the heir to the throne should be your first concern. Don't worry about the council. Your father and I will represent you and your plans."

"But you don't have the numbers!"

"Neither do we have the numbers when you're there."

"But . . ."

He shook his head. "I know these types of men. They always say no to everything at first. But if they give me the chance to explain, I'm sure they will see the wisdom, or at least enough of them will for the plan to pass."

"But I want to do it!" It was *her* idea.

"I understand. For now, be calm and quiet. You'll get your chance." He smiled and went back into the room.

Johanna went back to the living quarters, still clutching her papers. She was seething inside. She should have screamed at them. She should have told them that she wasn't going anywhere.

And then what?

These powerful men could easily make her life impossible.

And it was not as if she hadn't known that this was coming. Fighting it was useless because, though she might be the queen, these men had much more power than she did.

She guessed she'd have to resign herself to a lifetime of battles for the city. Master Deim and Father alone could never sway the council to go ahead with her plan.

While she stood there, a guard came towards her in the corridor, followed by a middle-aged woman who was taller than him.

Helena of Karathos must have been a striking beauty in her youth. She had long legs, long arms and slender fingers. She was probably in her late forties now. Johanna had never seen her in her prime, but apparently before the fires, there were still days when sailors were said to have big fights over her.

Not so much anymore. Her eyes were still dark, her eyebrows heavy and her hair—or whatever was left of it— raven black. These days, it was not so glossy anymore, occupied as she must be with tending the weeping burn wounds on the right side of her face.

"It's getting better," she said previously when Johanna had asked about it. "I keep it clean and more of the wound scabs over."

Her injuries would leave her with permanent ugly scars and must hurt, Johanna guessed, but Helena hadn't come here to talk about that.

"She's not far off," she said in her dark voice with thick accent. "Maybe tonight, maybe tomorrow, maybe next week. Not much longer than that. The child is big and she is very uncomfortable. It's the first one for her, yes?"

Johanna nodded, feeling uncomfortable.

"Call me when her pains start. I will come."

Johanna offered Helena some tea, but she said she needed to go to another woman with pains, so she left quickly.

Johanna strode into her office. She was tempted to slam the door, but that would seem childish.

Women were only good for producing heirs. It had always been that way and it was pointless to fight it.

With tears in her eyes, Johanna pushed the pile of draft letters aside. They would never be sent. There would not be investment in Saardam. There would be wars. Li Fai would not have his office. She would never see the little dragon again, never learn about her magic. Everything she had done was pointless. Her life was pointless.

She went to the window, leaning her forehead against the cool glass.

The royal office looked out over the former rose garden, and while there were signs that Roald had been working on a garden bed, he, and the guard who would accompany him, were nowhere to be seen.

From her position, Johanna could see the ravaged glass doors of the garden room. Throughout autumn and winter, the room had lain open to the elements. Dust and leaves had blown in, staining the floor and walls, causing mould to grow on the curtains. Animals had roosted in there, and bandits had camped there. The room would need a great deal of work before it was beautiful again.

Johanna left the room and went into the garden.

The air was warm and smelled of grass and flowers. Queen Cygna's rose beds were badly overgrown with weeds. There were dandelions and poppies, cornflowers and daisies, wild carrots and a variety of garden plants that had run riot, like foxgloves and lupins.

When Alexandre's henchmen took away the statue of the Triune that used to stand on a pedestal in the middle of the pond, they had knocked down the wall that used to be on the river side of the garden. Some of the rubble still lay in the garden beds. Last autumn's floods had invaded the garden beds on that side and washed away the soil that, Johanna had been told, the queen had brought in because the clay of the riverbank was too gluggy to grow roses. Now the garden bled into the reed beds and was more ideal for Roald than the old garden had ever been.

Johanna went to the old gazebo. The vandals had set fire to the roof, but the stone pillars that supported the roof still stood and the vandals had not been able to move the stone seats.

She sat down on a bench with a seat warmed by the sun.

The presence of the king was only indicated by the two palace guards who stood in front of the reed beds, while a group of courtiers hovered around a table that evidently contained Roald's morning tea in which he took little interest, as usual. Johanna had told them repeatedly not to bother, but they insisted that the king "had to eat well" and was "much too thin". Yes to both accounts, but trying to get Roald to do it was an effort that was best spent at the dinner table.

Johanna went to the table and took a cake from the plate held out to her by the courtier.

She was just about to join Father whom she spotted on another bench when there was a shout from the reeds, the tone of the voice distressed.

The guards looked at each other and frowned. Johanna looked at Father. The courtiers gasped.

"Was that His Majesty?"

The guards had already taken off into the reed bed.

Johanna called out, "Roald. What's going on?"

He would not answer that of course. He never did.

Johanna ploughed into the reeds after the guards. There was a narrow path where Roald usually walked. The ground was pretty soggy and she had to step carefully from one patch of flattened reeds to the next so her shoes didn't sink into the mud. Her dress snagged on sticks that had washed up during the flood.

"Roald!" she called.

Something went, "Eeeeh! Eeeeeh!" in the reeds.

That sounded like his voice.

"Roald!"

A courtier caught up with her. The man ran past her through the reed bed with a splosh-splosh-splosh and disappeared into the greenery in the direction of the river.

There was another shout, this time from one of the guards at the front.

Johanna hesitated. The ground got *very* wet here. More mud and puddle than dry land, really.

She kicked off her shoes off and continued clumsily. The reeds were hard to walk on with her soft feet. The water was cold and the mud squished—eeew—between her toes.

The hem of her dress got wet. She could see glimpses of the courtier's back between the reeds. He was heaving something heavy.

By the Triune, Roald was all right, was he?

But his voice was still going, "Eeeeh! Eeeeeh!"

He did that when he was distressed. He would be swaying, his eyes wide. She had to get to him quickly, to comfort him.

The courtier blocked her path. "No, Your Majesty. You shouldn't see this in your condition."

"The king needs my help." She was already getting tired of the *in your condition* that her close maids, courtiers and guards used as excuse to make her sit still and do nothing. That would only get worse.

"I will bring the king to you. Wait here."

The man turned around. She could see Roald's legs in between the reeds behind him. He was sitting in the water and looked indeed to be swaying and crying. The courtier tried to pull him up, but he squealed even more.

No, he wasn't going to come if the man was going to force him like that. He'd only scream and roll on the ground, and then he'd be all wet and muddy and everyone in the palace would talk about it for days.

Never mind waiting here, and whatever she shouldn't be seeing *in her condition*. In the past year she had seen so many awful things, there wasn't much that could still upset her. She followed the little path through ankle-deep water, holding up her dress. Her bare feet grew numb with the cold.

At the end of the path, where the reed bed made way for shallow water, one of the guards stood looking at a large and pale thing that lay in the water that was just deep enough to cover it. It took Johanna a few seconds to realise what she was seeing Pale grey cloth waved gently in the lapping water. An open hand reached for the sky.

Johanna raised her hand to her mouth.

A body, the form distorted by ripples in the water. A man, someone well-clad. As far as she could tell age on dead bodies, he looked quite young, had blond hair that floated about his face. His eyes were half open. His nose and chin were the only things that broke the surface, but water lapped in and out of his mouth.

She knew him. It was Auguste LaFontaine, the young nobleman who, just a few months ago, had been his family's message boy when they were trying to get Father to marry into their family.

Johanna stared, feeling sick. Roald was still squealing, but his voice sounded far off.

How did he end up here? She could see no sign of violence on him.

He'd drowned.

She was taken back to two nights ago, when she had clearly heard the splash of the man who had fallen or jumped into the water from the *Lady Sara*'s deck. She and Li Fai had looked, but hadn't been able to see anyone. The harbour was upstream from here.

Auguste LaFontaine had been snooping around on Father's ship?

A bunch of court guards splashed up behind her.

"Let us deal with that, Your Majesty," said the guard captain. He gently pulled her back to the reed bed.

Roald was still squealing, swaying, clamping his hands over his face.

Johanna crouched next to him. "Listen to me." She took his wrists and forced him to sit still.

He still resisted her, trying to keep swaying against her grip.

"Sit still! Maybe you like getting wet, but I don't"

He relaxed a bit. She was able to pull his hands away from his face. His eyes were still wide. Sweat glistened on his forehead.

He squealed, "There is a ghost in the water!"

"It's not a ghost, but someone has died."

"He's all white. Did you see that? He's all white. He's been touched by magic!"

"It's just the colour that skin goes when someone is dead and the body lies in the water."

"The frogs! What did he do to the frogs?"

"It doesn't bother the frogs."

"But the frogs will be scared!"

"Come, Roald. Get up. You'll catch a cold."

She heaved herself up and pulled him up with her. A guard rushed to help. A couple of others splashed into the water and gathered around the body, staring, speculating what he'd been doing there.

Johanna and Roald made their way back to the garden, where courtiers came to help them. It seemed that the commotion had caused the meeting of the King's Council to be halted. The men had also come into the garden. They stood on the grass, looking out of place in their finery and out of their element in the sunshine.

Father rushed up to her. "Dear daughter of mine, what is going on? Are you all right?"

Johanna told him.

His eyes widened. "Auguste LaFontaine?"

"I'm wondering if it was him we disturbed at the *Lady Sara* two nights ago."

Johanna should go inside with Roald. He was wet and shivering. When he had an attack like that, he was usually very tired, but the guards were now carrying the body out of the reeds into the garden. They put Auguste down on the grass. His body had gone rigid. His arm stood out at an angle as if he was pointing at something.

The chief guard who stood next to Johanna judged that he'd been in the water for no more than two days.

"He doesn't float yet," he said in a tone that suggested he had experience in this matter.

Johanna wasn't sure if she wanted to know this much detail. She felt ill.

One of the guards gestured to his superior.

"Excuse me, Your Majesties." The chief guard went to join his men who bent or crouched over the body.

Father went and had a look as well, and then he gestured for Johanna to come, too.

Dragging him through the reeds had twisted Auguste's shirt and exposed the soft underside of his lower arm, where the skin was marked with an ink stain about the length of her thumb, in the shape of a dragon.

The same symbol as the carving that Li Fai had given her.

CHAPTER 11

JOHANNA QUICKLY TOOK Roald into the bedroom, and then she went to look for Nellie. She had to tell the whole story over again, also about seeing the man on the *Lady Sara* a few nights ago.

Nellie's mouth fell open. "But why would he be sneaking around on your father's ship, Mistress Johanna?"

"Wouldn't it be good if we knew that?"

There were many possible reasons why Auguste might have been walking over the deck, maybe spying on Li Han's iron ship next to the *Lady Sara*. Maybe to do damage to Father's business.

A chill went over her.

The door opened and a courtier came in. "Your Majesty, your father wants to see you in the Red Room."

"I'm coming." Johanna looked at Nellie. "Are you going to be all right with Roald?"

"I just give him the usual treatment?"

"Yes. Give him warm milk with honey and books about frogs. Lots of frogs."

Nellie assured that she would look after Roald, who was

already going through the shelves for a book to read, and Johanna went to the Red Room, where Father sat on the couch close to the hearth.

"I've asked Li Han to come," he said. His expression was grave. "Some members of the King's Council will be here, too."

Johanna's heart skipped a beat. "Do you really think Li Han has something to do with this?"

"I don't know. I don't think so. At least, I hope not." But he was worried, clearly. "Some people suggested to me that Li Han may try to get rid of all his competition who are trying to build the iron ships and that he's here and wants an office for that reason: that he is looking for ways to kill his competitors or ruin their businesses. I don't think that is true at all, but now that this has happened, I don't know how I'll be able to defend my position."

A deep hole of despair opened up in Johanna's mind. "If we had a water magician, we'd know what happened." Or at least they would know whether Auguste had been pushed or jumped and simply met with misfortune while sneaking around in a place where he wasn't supposed to be.

"If I'm correct, I heard you mention a water magician." Master Deim had come into the room. "I am not sure how that would help. A water magician can tell how he ended up in the water, but it might just have been too dark to see who was chasing the fellow or why he jumped."

Johanna gave him a sharp look. That was as close an admission she'd heard from him that *he*, in fact, was a water magician. "Chasing?"

"He jumped off the *Lady Sara*'s deck. He tried to swim, but the current was too strong and he got swept out of the harbour. Shouldn't have attempted to flee that way while the tide was going out."

"There was nowhere else for him to go, because we were on the quay."

"It was still stupid. The water is too cold. I don't think he was a good swimmer."

"What about the mark on his skin?"

Master Deim shook his head. "I have no idea. He must already have had it when he got into the water, but not too long before that. It's drawing ink. It would come off within a few days."

"So, what? We disturbed him at the *Lady Sara* where he was doing something mysterious, he tried to swim, but drowned? That doesn't account for the mark on his arm."

While they were speaking Johan Delacoeur had come in, followed by Thomas Kloostermans and Joris Decamp.

"The matter seems clear to me," Thomas said. "This eastern stranger captured him, gave him this mark, and then he jumped when escaping."

"It's a warning," Johan Delacoeur said, nodding.

Johanna protested. "That doesn't make sense. If that were the case, Auguste would have run to us and not from us. Also why would Li Han capture this man? Why would he draw in ink on his skin?"

"Evil magical foreign ways," Thomas said, his voice dark. "Who knows why these people do things? It's only a matter of time before the dragon comes out of that ship and roams the city. And you will all be sorry when all I can say is, 'I told you so.'"

"Oh, stop it with your stupid superstition!" Master Deim called out. "We're trying to solve a crime here. The witch hunts have long gone."

"Tell me with an honest face that you truly believe that these people have no evil magic."

"No *evil* magic," Master Deim said, his voice soft. "I believe that."

"You are wrong! *All* magic of this type is evil." Thomas Kloosterman's eyes looked like they were about to pop out of his head.

A chill went over Johanna's back. It was unlikely that Li Fai's little dragon was as harmless as it had looked. She said, "That is all very well, but why would Li Han purposely put this mark on Auguste's arm and then kill him to advertise what he's done? Why would he even want this young man dead?"

"I have no idea, but we can ask him right now." Thomas gestured to the door where a courtier had come in.

The man confirmed, "The eastern trader is here."

"Do let him in," Master Deim said.

The courtier disappeared again, and a man came into the room, flanked by two massive guards who each wore armour and looked dangerous despite having left their weapons at the door. The much slenderer man in between them was not Li Han, but his son.

The guards accompanied him to the middle of the room, where they stopped and let their master walk to the throne alone. Li Fai bowed before Johanna. "Your Majesty, it is always an honour to see you."

Johanna cringed at seeing the smile in his eyes.

Today Li Fai was wearing a white shirt with a brocade jacket over the top. His hair was tied in a sleek bun at the back of his head.

He remained standing in a bowed position.

"Do get up," she said, glancing at the nobles.

He did, meeting her eyes. He was so serious. Doing his job. Representing his father's company.

"I'm afraid I don't have a pleasant reason for calling you here." She cringed.

"Oh?"

"I will show you. Come."

She led him into the corridor.

He walked next to her, his footsteps silent like a cat's.

They went into the bare, damaged ballroom. Alexandre had made a start at cleaning up this room, but hadn't progressed any further than to clean up and repair the doors to the garden room. That particular room was still in its ruined state. The guards had placed the body on the stone floor.

They gathered in a circle around it—Father, Master Deim, the three men from the King's Council and a couple of guards, including Li Fai's.

Li Fai's face did not show any emotion at the sight of the drowned man. He looked puzzled until she pointed out the ink mark on his arm. Then his eyes widened briefly.

"This is the mark of your family. Do you know anything about how this came to be on the man's arm?"

"You think I did this? Why would I put this stamp on a man's body?"

"I'm presuming it was put on before he entered the water from our ship two nights ago. Right now, I'm not drawing any conclusions about who put it on or why."

Thomas Kloostermans snorted.

Li Fai's gaze shifted from her to Father, to the three nobles and back. "The brand is for marking our merchandise. It's not for people."

"You draw this sign on your products?"

"Yes. It's a stamp. We use it to put on bags and crates."

"You're certain that you or your crew did not put it on this man?"

"No. It's for things, not people. It's a stamp, not a brand. You put it in ink and stamp it on bags. We don't trade in slaves."

"Do you keep the stamp in a place where someone could steal it and use it?"

He frowned. "It is usually in a cabin on the deck of our ship."

"Would you miss it if someone took it for half a day or a day and put it back later?"

"Depends on if we need it. Some days the cargo manager doesn't use it."

"Did he use the stamp yesterday?"

"No. He only uses it if stock is loaded or unloaded. He keeps it in a box with a pot of ink and an ink pad."

"Could someone have stolen it?"

He gave her an affronted look. "That's why we have the ducks."

Yes, he had told her about them. "However, it looks like someone has used this stamp."

"I don't know how. The ducks always make a noise when anything moves on the deck. There are always people on the wharf. I don't know how anyone could have taken the stamp." His voice had lost the even tone, and his accent became more pronounced. "We have nothing to do with this man. I don't know why he jumped. I came to the quay to check. We have not spoken to him. I have never seen him before. I don't know who he is."

Johanna cringed inside.

Li Fai gaze's darted from one person to the other. His eyes were pleading when they met Johanna's.

Johanna said, "If you haven't done this, who would have?"

"I don't know." He glanced at the nobles again, and back to Johanna.

"Have people made threats to you or your family recently?"

"Yes. But that is normal. It happens wherever we go. People don't like us or our ship, and they make threats."

"Who are these people in Saardam?"

"I don't know them. They don't show themselves. They

write letters. Sometimes there is a fake name on them, most of the time not. They tell my father to leave. They tell him that he will be killed. It's the same everywhere. We get used to it."

That was a rather terrible way to live.

"But talk and trying to scare us is easy. Writing letters like a coward is easy. Doing the things they threaten is not. My grandfather always says that. Words are easy but deeds are not. Sometimes people try to steal things from us, or yell bad words at our crew, but we get used to that. This . . ." He nodded at the dead man—

"Can you swear to us that you have nothing to do with the mark on this man's arm?"

"Yes, I swear. I have not seen this man. I have not touched this man. I have nothing to do with him."

Johanna believed him.

The three men from the King's Council watched with unemotional faces. Johanna didn't think that they believed him.

It was rather macabre holding council with a dead body between them, and the waft of wet clothes mixed with the beginnings of decay did nothing to calm Johanna's queasy stomach, so she led the group into the foyer, where the rest of Li Fai's entourage waited.

"Well," Johanna said to him. "I am still interested in your plan for an office, but we first need to establish to the satisfaction of the King's Council that neither you nor anyone in your crew have any responsibility for the death of this man."

He nodded. The expression in his eyes of confusion, bewilderment and hurt disturbed Johanna deeply. He spoke the truth, she was sure of that. Not only that, she wanted him to teach her magic.

He bowed and left with his entourage. Johanna looked at his back until he had gone through the palace gates.

"How do we know that he's speaking the truth?" Johan Delacoeur said. "If it's true what he is saying about the ducks, then the only people who could have had access to the deck at times when no one else was there were the members of his crew."

"Auguste LaFontaine is a son of a respected family," Thomas Kloostermans said. "I'm sure the family will be highly affronted if he stands accused of larceny. It's most inappropriate."

"I told you my version of the story," Johanna said. And she very much wanted to challenge the respectability of the LaFontaine family. Or, for that matter, that of some other "well-respected" families.

Thomas waggled his eyebrows. "If the man you saw jump in the water was indeed Auguste."

"It was," Master Deim said, his voice firm. Thank the Triune for Master Deim.

"How do you know?" Thomas shifted his gaze, lifting his chin.

"I know. I saw him." Master Deim kept a straight face. He crossed his arms over his chest and gave Thomas a cold stare. *Magic* was the answer, and Thomas would know it. That was the crux of the matter. As a staunch supporter of the Belaman Church, Thomas Kloostermans would support only the type of magic sanctioned by the church, and opinions over exactly what sort of magic that was varied wildly.

He snorted. "To me, it is clear. That gold brought by the slitty-eyed stranger has bewitched you, and your words are muddled by it. This man and his family are trying to scare us with magic. This is what Alexandre was trying to protect us from. He was doing it poorly and angered a lot of people—"

Johanna burst out. " 'Angered' does not quite cover the fact that he killed many people and burned their houses!"

Thomas lowered his voice. "I didn't say he was skilful or

good. I said he was trying to protect the land from the influence of foul dragon magic, and match the menace of the iron ships with iron ships of our own. This murder of a son of one of our respected noble families proves that the threat is real, and that these people are not here to our benefit." He sounded like he was speaking through clenched teeth and made a point of looking at her stomach.

Johanna responded equally terse. "They are here for business. We have to do business with them, or they will do business with Anglia." Why was that so hard for these men to understand?

"If he can prove that he's got nothing to do with this death," Master Deim said. "But I don't think that will be too hard."

Thomas Kloostermans glared at him. "So you believe."

"I *know* that. But rest assured, the palace guards will investigate and they will find out what happened."

It seemed that there was no more to be said.

Thomas Kloostermans huffed something about being busy and excused himself. Johanna watched him go down the steps into the forecourt.

Johan Delacoeur nodded to her. "My congratulations on the impending birth. I don't think anyone has said this to you today."

"Well, thank you." The next thing he would start talking about how she should rest and do only womanly things like embroidery, so she changed the subject. "I don't think anyone has been in the mood for congratulations. It's a dark day."

"If you ask me, Your Majesty, I'd say that Auguste was asking for trouble. If he was snooping around the eastern trader's ship and one of those mountainous deck hands pushed him over the side, it could only have been his own fault."

"But they didn't, and he fell off the deck of the *Lady Sara.*

Li Fai came to check because he heard a noise. That was the only time he became involved."

"If you say so."

"I was there."

"We'll see." Clearly he didn't believe her. Was there anything more frustrating than dealing with these men who thought she made things up?

He dipped his head to her and also left.

The next person in line, Joris Decamp, came up to her. "I'm sorry to bother you, Your Majesty, but the LaFontaine family is asking me a lot of questions, mainly about getting access to the body so they can hold a funeral."

"They can come to pick him up." Everyone who needed to have seen the dragon mark had seen it.

"They also told me that they launched their own investigation. They're not happy with what they called our lax approach."

"They're not happy that we haven't gone and arrested Li Han and put him in jail?"

He gave her a penetrating look. "Many people question your trust in the eastern trader. They don't understand why you believe his words and disregard the words of the town's citizens."

By "people" of course he meant nobles. Those came with the agenda of defending the city against the eastern menace and the evil church.

Normally, Joris Decamp tended to support her, but this made it clear how fragile her position was. They tolerated her because of Roald, because there was no one else to take the throne. As a woman, they were only willing to treat her seriously as long as she said womanly, obedient things.

The worst thing was that she was utterly dependent on them, and they now had control of everything and would destroy all her plans.

CHAPTER 12

JOHANNA MADE SOME sort of excuse and went to her office.

These men were going to destroy everything for the sake of their opinions. Just because they didn't like the church, and didn't like Li Han, and they were afraid that Li Han would put some of them out of business that they could have spent the past few months rebuilding, but hadn't.

Just because . . .

Because they were nobles and it was their sole purpose in life to stop her ideas. Because she was a woman. Because she was not a noble. Because she had saved the crown prince's life while they hoped he'd die, because she married him while their daughters thumbed their noses at him.

Because the *common citizens* of Saardam would benefit from her plan.

And though she didn't know how, she wasn't going to let them destroy her work.

She pulled a piece of parchment out of the drawer and spread it on the desk. Then she opened the pot of ink and selected a pen from the tray. Clearly, Roald had been rummaging in her writing things again, because there was charcoal in the tray. She'd already told him several times to keep it separate because it made everything black.

She wiped her hands on the dress—it was almost black anyway, dipped the pen in the ink and wrote:

To Li Fai. She hoped she spelled that correctly.

The events of today disturb me greatly, but I want you to know that I do not hold you or any of your crew in any way responsible for the death of this poor man. Some members of the King's Council may not believe you, but there is no doubt in my mind that you are speaking the truth.

She signed off with simply "Johanna" because anything else felt preposterous.

And then she added:

P.S. I very much enjoyed your openness in discussing magic. It is a difficult subject in this town because most people are afraid of it. I hope we can continue our discussion soon.

She let the letter dry for a moment and then rolled it up and sealed it before she could change her mind. She would not allow these nobles and church people to chase Li Han to Anglia, because he was innocent.

She went to the guard station and asked the young man there to see that it was delivered.

Next, Johanna went into the garden.

Most of Queen Cygna's rose bushes in the higher part of the garden had survived a year of neglect. Not having been pruned, they had become gangly, but the more hardy varieties were sprouting flowers. Johanna found a pair of pruning shears in the tool shed and set about cutting flowers that had just opened. A courtier came to ask what she was doing, and she informed him that she was cutting flowers for the poor man's funeral, and that reply seemed to satisfy him.

It was a bit strange being in the garden while Roald was inside. The flower baskets that she retrieved from the garden shed showed her images of Roald pottering about with jars and buckets. In one vision, a green frog climbed over the edge of a pot and jumped to the ground. Roald ran after it over the lawn. It made her laugh.

She divided the roses between the two baskets and took them inside.

Then she called for Nellie, who came to see her in the office, frowning at the roses.

"I want you to do something for me." Johanna took one basket. "For this basket, I want you to find some jam or compote from the cellar, or some spices or tobacco from Father's store. I want you to take it to the Nieland family with my apologies for forgetting Octavio's birthday."

"But that was two months ago."

"Yes. I've forgotten it."

Nellie frowned at her. Johanna could almost see her thoughts trying to work out whether she was serious or not.

She picked up the other basket. "To this one, you will add a little singlet and a blanket or some such and take it to Josefina LaFontaine, who I understand has given birth to a girl." She picked up a notebook from the desk. "Give her this, too. Tell her that I want Josefina to teach the girl how to read. And give the flowers for her cousin's funeral."

Nellie nodded, but she still look confused.

"When you visit these families, you will leave the entire basket there, and a couple of days later, we'll send someone around to collect the empty basket."

Nellie gasped and raised her hand to her mouth. Now she understood. "But Mistress Johanna, you can't go snooping on people like that. Why would you do this? You said you'd finished with this . . . magic."

"There are things I need to know."

"Why not leave the investigation to the guards?"

"There are things no one will tell the guards—especially

the women, because I bet the guards will be hesitant to question the noble ladies."

"But you can't just . . . eavesdrop on those families—"

"Yes, we can. A man has died. Another man has hurt his wife. Yet another man has threatened someone in the street about something they are looking for. I have suspicions that these things could be related."

"You are speaking in riddles, Mistress Johanna."

"Has the shepherd been here?"

Nellie blinked at the sudden change of subject. "No, he hasn't. It's very strange—"

"Then we will send him a basket, too."

"Mistress Johanna! You don't spy on the shepherd!"

"Just do it, Nellie. Unless Greetje is ready to go back home, but I don't think she should until we know what's going on."

"No, she won't. Not yet. She's not been feeling well. I think her pains will start very soon."

"Then go to him and tell him that. Deliver a basket with some singlets and a blanket."

Nellie nodded, looking unhappy. "I really thought you were finished with this wood magic. I mean, that horrible thing that happened to the poor man having his life squeezed out of him by a tree would have been enough to put everyone off. Of course he is an evil man, but did he deserve to die like that?"

"Nellie, you never cease to surprise me with your capacity to judge people kindly."

"It's what the Triune teaches us to do. I'm a forgiving person, because holding grudges just makes you horrible and grumpy."

"But, you're talking about Alexandre. . . ."

"A horrible man, by all accounts, but like all people,

deserved to be treated with dignity, because when you start treating people poorly, that is the end of the world."

"Then, Nellie, if you feel like that about what I asked you to do, I can ask someone else to go."

Nellie's eyes widened in shock. "No, Mistress Johanna. I would never allow that!"

"But you just said . . ."

"What you tell me to do is what I do. You are much wiser than I am and I trust that you ask me for a good reason. To be perfectly honest, Mistress Johanna, and don't tell anyone I said this, those horrible arrogant families could do with being taught a lesson."

Johanna laughed, and then turned serious again. "As long as no one dies."

"Yes." Nellie nodded.

Johanna sighed. "I'm sorry to ask you to do this, but you know most times I feel that you're the only friend I have. If . . ." She shuddered. "When the time comes that the pains start and the child is about to arrive, you are the only person I want with me, besides Helena."

Nellie looked at her with wide eyes. "Oh!" And then her eyes glittered. "Oh, Mistress Johanna!" She wiped her eyes with the end of her sleeve. "Look at that. You're making me cry."

"It's true," Johanna said.

"Oh, mistress Johanna!" Nellie wiped at her eyes again.

Johanna's eyes pricked, too. Words about how scared she was of the pains were on her tongue. Or about how she was almost certain that Roald was not the father of this child. Kylian had made a pass at Nellie. She would understand how overwhelming his magic was.

Johanna also asked Nellie to collect any wood that she could find from the warehouses and quayside near the *Lady Sara* and Li Han's ship. She drew a map of the part of the quay and indicated spots where there might be wooden items that could tell her a story.

"You have to write down precisely where you collected them," she told Nellie.

Some of the places would require a man to visit without raising eyebrows, like the inside of the warehouses. Nellie said that any of the groundsmen would be happy to go if she asked.

"I don't want people to get into trouble," Johanna said.

"People are happy to take risks. They adore you, mistress Johanna."

Nellie took her task seriously. She wanted to know if the type of wood mattered. Johanna explained that willow wood was the best, but any other wood would do. She said the best things were items that weren't used too often. Things like tables and benches typically only told stories one day old, because they were used so much, and newer memories took the place of older ones.

By the time the maid came in, wondering why Johanna hadn't called for the coach, she realised that not only had she forgotten to get dressed, she was going to be late to church.

CHAPTER 13

NELLIE GASPED WHEN she realised that. "Oh, mistress Johanna, how terrible! Quickly, I'll help you get ready."

"No, Nellie."

Nellie stared at her, eyes wide. "What do you mean, no?"

"I've been thinking about this. We have Greetje here and the shepherd hasn't even been to visit his wife. Is that an example of a caring man or one who is sorry about what he has done? Even before this happened, I've been very concerned about the way the shepherd has been preaching in church. It's like he's gone mad, like he's trying to get people to sign up to go to war. You can't make magic go away by ignoring it. He should know that better than anyone. Something has happened that has made him act like this and I don't think we should give him any more power than he already has until he calms down and we find out what it is."

"He's afraid of magic."

"He's a wind magician. Everyone knows that. I don't understand what is going on with him. You know, I have looked in the *Book of Verses* but can't see where it says that magic is forbidden."

"But even Shepherd Romulus used to say this."

"Yes, but I don't think the couple of verses that he always quotes mean what he thinks they mean. The most important quote is two lines from *The Book of Revelation* that say, '*And those whose magic turns to evil, let them burn in doom.*' The church of the Triune interprets this as meaning 'no magic', but the Belaman Church uses the same version of *The Book of Revelations* and they interpret it differently. The church has always fought their own battles about magic. The Belaman Church uses the word magic to mean belief, for the holy teachings. Shepherd Romulus would have been talking about that type of magic."

"I don't know, Mistress Johanna. It all seems very confusing to me. None of these supposedly important men ever seem to say what they actually mean. If they talk about a woman's 'situation' they mean she's with child. If they talk about 'magic' they really mean the belief of the Belaman Church?"

"Our shepherd doesn't. He definitely means real magic."

"But Shepherd Romulus didn't?"

"I don't think so. After all, true magic is not common in Saardam. He received his teaching from the great seminary in Lurezia."

Nellie sighed and shook her head. "It's all so complicated. But for what it's worth, I think that the church would be a bad enemy to have."

"It is, but instead of going to the nightly service—because how much gossip would I start by coming in late—"

"Less than by not going at all?"

"I don't know about that. But anyway, I don't want to disturb the service and call attention to myself, so I'm going to light a candle for Auguste LaFontaine in the Belaman Church—"

Nellie gasped.

"Mother used to go the Belaman Church. I could call myself a member even if I haven't been baptised. I think you taught me something today about treating someone with dignity, even if it's someone you don't like and who hasn't treated you with dignity. Next time Auguste's family come into the church for the funeral, they will see a candle with a card that has a royal seal and they'll know that I sympathise with their loss. And also, Nellie, just because the old bearded men of the Belaman Church don't like the Church of the Triune and declare that it's no longer part of their church, that doesn't mean we have to agree with that. As far as I know, they teach the same things and fight against the same evil magic, even if they use different names for it. Anyway, after I've lit the candle, I'll go and pray in shepherd Carolus' church. They don't have evening services, so I can enter there without disturbing anything."

So it was done.

The home of the Belaman Church, the small but ornate building around the corner from the marketplace, had "miraculously" survived the fires. The Holy Father Fabricius was Burovian. He spoke with a thick accent that noble children often mocked—and got clipped on the ear for doing so.

Johanna used to go to this church to pick up her mother. In those days, the streets seemed so much more colourful.

Her early memories were of walking down the street on Father's hand and seeing people stream out of the little building of the Belaman Church. There had been a wedding and all the guests were dressed in vibrant colours. Some of the women wore costumes that included headbands with hundreds of dangling coins. They were colourful people, mostly dark-haired and olive-skinned. Several men were playing lutes while the happy couple, both in cream-coloured silk, stood on the church steps.

Whatever happened to that Saardam?

Those people must have left, too, gone to Lurezia or any of the big towns.

Johanna alighted from the coach in front of the building. It looked smaller than she remembered, and had recently been cleaned.

She went up the steps and pushed the door. It creaked.

Johanna peeked in. The noise brought no reaction from inside. Candles flapped in sconces attached to the pillars that supported the roof.

Johanna took a candle from the box on a table in the foyer and dropped a Phoenician gold coin in the donations box.

She then walked down the aisle. There was such a difference between this church and the wooden building of the Church of the Triune. The walls behind the altar and along the sides were covered in brightly painted murals depicting scenes from the *Book of Verses*. There was a lot of gold and blue paint, and neither of those colours was cheap. Almost every side panel of the outer wall told its own story. Sometimes there would be a statue or a little altar dedicated to this or that saint. The floor displayed elaborate mosaics.

She couldn't help but think of the splendid building in Florisheim where she had prayed to the saint Magdalena whom the people in Florisheim worshipped as saint of mothers and children. And the saint had granted Johanna her prayers. Even if Roald's seed didn't work, the saint had granted Johanna a child.

She placed the candle on the tiered shelves where other candles burned and leaked wax all over the wood. She inserted her card in the groove in the wood that ran along the front edge of the shelf. *In the memory of Auguste LaFontaine, in sympathy with those who mourn his loss. Queen Johanna Carmine de Lacoeur van Leeuwen Brouwer.*

She knelt on the bench and said a few words of prayer.

Only when she rose again did she become aware of the dark-robed figure kneeling at a bench in front of the giant mural of the Lord Saviour. The mural depicted Him as a bearded man. His friendly face had always fascinated her as a child.

The man who sat on his knees was the Holy Father Fabricius.

How long had he been sitting there?

He didn't look up, but sat with his head down, his hands folded in prayer. Johanna sat on the frontmost pew and waited until he raised his head.

"It is a good thing to see you here, Your Highness."

"I came to light a candle for the poor young man who drowned in the harbour."

He nodded. "It's so sad."

"Tell the family that I sympathise with them." She rose and stepped into the aisle.

He dipped his head. "It is terrible. Magic stirs in the belly of this town. Every time something bad happens, I tell the citizens: there will be death and destruction until you vanquish this foul magic."

His eyes were intense.

Johanna nodded a lame agreement and retreated down the aisle, remembering suddenly why she had started attending the Church of the Triune's services. The Holy Father Fabricius always said things like this, as if it were his task to make everyone afraid.

The coach that waited in front of the church then took her to the much smaller church building two streets away that was the home of Shepherd Carolus.

He was a much more cheerful fellow and came to Johanna

with open arms when she entered. Since coming back to Saardam with him, he had tamed his straw-like hair, but he was as tall and gangly as ever.

"Welcome, welcome. I feared we'd never see you again in this humble building. Come and share a prayer to the Holy Father."

They did. Because all things in the church came in threes, Johanna dedicated her prayer first to Auguste LaFontaine, then to Roald in the hope that he wouldn't remain scarred by finding the body and then to Li Fai *because he is innocent and doesn't deserve all this trouble.*

"What brings you here today?" Shepherd Carolus asked when they finished.

"I want to ask you something."

"Ask away."

"Tell me if it's an inappropriate thing to ask or if you don't want to talk about it. I'm asking this as a citizen with concern for the safety of our city."

The laughter faded from his face.

"Apparently, when he came to Saardam, Li Han brought in the hold of his ship a crate that had been given to him by a monk in Seneza to be delivered to Shepherd Victor. It seems that many people are keen to get their hands on whatever is inside. Word goes that the shepherd doesn't have it, but no one knows where it is."

"Oh, he has it all right."

"What is inside?"

Shepherd Carolus sighed and shook his head. The serious look on his face didn't suit him terribly well. "Rumours abound about this thing. Word goes that when the Most Holy Father Severino of the Belaman Church made the decision to cast the Church of the Triune out, he also no longer wished to hold onto the relics that the Church of the Triune had trusted him with."

"Did he have any of our relics?" This was the first she heard of it.

"There is some discussion over that. The Church as we know it and we practice here . . ." He gestured around the empty pews. ". . . is quite a new thing, but apparently the forebears of the Church of the Triune arose in poor farming communities in the area where Saarland, Estland, Burovia and Gelre join. Those poor people are very much into relics because they have so little and treasure each possession."

Johanna nodded. She had seen the heartbreaking poverty of those people and the incredibly poor land they farmed, and where the father was happy to receive coin from bandits seeking pleasure with his daughter.

"It is said, but I don't know how true any of this is, that the early shepherds came from that area and brought their relics, which were later transferred to the Belaman Church for safekeeping."

Johanna frowned. "But they're objects, things made out of wood or stone. Or bones. How can they be more valuable than gold?"

But as she said that, she already knew the answer: they were objects to which *magic* was ascribed.

Shepherd Carolus continued, "Other people say that the relics didn't belong to the church but to some ancient pagan settlement which died out. They say that the relics impart witchcraft on those who have them. And other people again say that this crate is something sent by the Red Baron under the guise of being a religious relic in order to bring about our destruction."

"Now *that* is something I can believe."

"Whatever it is, Shepherd Victor has the crate."

"At the church?"

"I don't know. I've asked him if he wants help in dealing with it, but he keeps changing the subject. If it were something simple, he would have dealt with it. I don't think it's simple, which goes against the most obvious answer: that the contents are sent by the Baron purely with ill intent. In that case, the shepherd could just toss the crate in the fire and be done with it. I think there *are* relics of some description involved."

"What sort of things would relics be?"

"It could be anything. Many of the old relics are not pleasant things. I've seen relics that are necklaces made of human teeth. Some relics are the bones or scales of strange animals. There is usually a horrible story related to the relic, and many are objects of dark magic and shouldn't be disturbed for that reason, especially not in here in Saardam, where some like to think we have no magic."

"Could one turn a magic relic harmless?"

"I guess you could. I guess that might be what he's trying to do."

"Or destroy it?"

"Hmmm. A magic relic would unleash terrible powers if you tried to destroy it. You'd have to be very careful that you didn't end up with a worse situation than when you started. But again, I don't know much about it, much less about what's inside that box that he's got. But one thing I want to say. He loves that girl and would never harm her. If this thing made him do that, then it's something terrible indeed."

After some small talk with the shepherd—and it was good to see him again—Johanna went back to the palace.

She needed something to eat before going to see Greetje, but as she sat in the kitchen, Nellie came in, carrying a pile of bedsheets, her face red.

"Oh mistress, there you are. I've called Helena. Greetje is complaining about cramps."

CHAPTER 14

JOHANNA ARRIVED AT Greetje's room at the same time that Helena came out. She shook her head in response to Johanna's unasked question. "Not yet, but she is very close. I'll come back tomorrow morning."

"Can I go in?"

"Yes, of course."

Johanna went into the room. Greetje sat in the bed, nibbling at a slice of bread that stood on a plate on the cover. Her stomach was so round and big that she had to lean back.

She looked at Johanna when she came in, but said nothing. Johanna sat down on the chair next to the bed. "How are you feeling?"

"I'm sick of this. I can't sleep, I can't walk, I can't sit, I can't breathe. Everything hurts. It's not fun at all."

Johanna could see that. "It won't last much longer."

"No." Greetje stared into the distance.

A moment of uneasy silence passed.

Then Johanna said, "I need to talk to you about something."

"Oh?" She turned to Johanna. There was a slightly alarmed look in those grey eyes.

"I asked you yesterday about a crate that your husband received. You said that you didn't know anything about it."

"I don't." The answer came a bit quick for her liking.

"Has he mentioned anything to you about it?"

"No. Not that I know."

"You're sure?"

"Yes, why do you keep asking?"

"Because it's important, because I think your husband might be in trouble."

"He's not hiding anything from anyone, if that's what you think."

Obviously, he was, and Johanna was unsure why Greetje was becoming so defensive on behalf of her husband who had mistreated her. "But at the same time you have to agree that he's not himself and that there has to be a reason. I spoke to Shepherd Carolus."

Greetje gave her a sharp look.

"He says that rumours are that following the verdict by the Most Holy Father Severino of the Belaman Church that the Church of the Triune can no longer be part of that organisation, he arranged to ship back to Shepherd Victor the relics of the church which had been held in safekeeping by the Belaman Church—"

"That's a lie."

"I didn't say it was the truth. It is what people are talking about on the streets. Failing better information, they consider it the truth."

"It's still a lie. The whole thing is a lie."

"For something that you say your husband doesn't have, you seem to know a good deal about it."

"He talked about it."

"Then what did he say?"

"Why is this so important? It's just a thing."

"There are many objects that are not *just a thing*. Is the king's crown *just a thing?* Is his Carmine Cloak *just a thing?* Or is a flag *just a thing?* And the statue of the Triune that Alexandre's men went to the effort to drag to the harbour and drop there, if that were *just a thing* do you think the church would have made such an effort to raise it and clean it?"

Greetje looked down at the bedspread. There was one piece of bread left on the plate that stood next to her, and she picked crumbs off the crust.

Johanna continued. "Things can be symbols, but worse, things can contain magic. I am beginning to suspect we're dealing with such a magical thing. If your husband is in any way as stubborn as he used to be when he worked for Father, he would not admit this. Because magic doesn't exist, according to the church—"

"I don't know what you're getting at. You're making underhanded comments about my husband. He's a good man."

"He may need help, Greetje, and he may be too stubborn to admit it. And something doesn't add up in all your tales. I don't think you're telling the entire truth of what happened."

"I am!" Her eyes were wide.

"Or you're leaving some key bits of information out. I don't know why and I don't need to know exactly what went on in your family, but tomorrow, I will be sending guards to your husband to ask him about it, because in the time you've been here, he has not once come to the palace to check on you. If you think like me, that's not normal, and if you think that he is going to tell the guards something that you haven't told me, that's not going to look good, is it?"

Greetje looked up at her. Tears welled in her eyes. "I don't know why everyone is so mean to me. I should have stayed at home."

Maybe you should. "You're tired, and maybe it's the wrong time to be worried about it. I'm going to write some letters. If you want me, I'll be in my office." Johanna rose.

"No. Don't go. I'm scared."

"The birth pains are a natural thing. Your body will know what to do." Helena always said this, anyway. Johanna felt terrible, because she was scared, too.

"No. It's not that."

"Then what?"

Greetje hesitated. Met Johanna's eyes. Looked down again. Then she said, her voice barely audible, "I looked."

Johanna went back to the chair next to the bed and sat down again. The child inside her was giving her a most unbecoming set of kicks.

Greetje continued, "That crate you were talking about? It's in his room upstairs, with all the skulls and the teeth and the other terrible things that he collected."

"Why did you say he didn't have it?"

"Because . . ." Greetje's lip trembled. "Because it is an evil thing. Because . . . he made me promise not to touch it or look at it . . . because . . ." She covered her face with her hands.

"What, Greetje?" Johanna's heart was thudding. "Because what?"

"Because . . . I couldn't help myself and I was stupid, and I looked anyway when I thought he wasn't watching . . ."

She burst out into tears, sobbing so hard that her words came out as incomprehensible wails. Johanna moved from the chair to the bed. Greetje fell into her arms, crying into her shoulder in long, gasping wails. Johanna patted her back.

"Why did you do it?" she asked when the worst seemed to have passed.

"Because I'm a stupid woman! He even told me that. But

honestly, this thing was calling out to me from the moment he brought it into the house."

Johanna shuddered, thinking of the twisted tree that held Alexandre prisoner that called out to her when she came to the market place. "So, what happened that you haven't already told me?"

"I've not told you any lies!"

"No, but you held back information."

Greetje's mouth twitched. After a short silence, she started in a low voice. "So he brought this thing home and as soon as he took it inside the door, I could feel its evil. I asked the old maid who has been with his family for years, but she said I was making it up. She always thinks I'm crazy. Then I asked my husband, and he said that it was something he needed to deal with, and that I shouldn't go into the room upstairs until he said it was safe. I was not to open the crate or look at it or have anything to do with it. That's when he started spending so much time there praying, and sometimes crying. And I really could not stand it anymore so I told him to take the thing out of the house, and he said he would but he didn't. I asked the maid to tell him the same thing, because he listens better to her than to me, and he got angry with me for pulling his trusted maid into it. And then I thought enough is enough, so one day when he was at church, I went into the room."

Her chin trembled. She took a big, shuddering breath.

"The crate stood on the table in the middle of the room. The lid was off, but I couldn't see into it from the door. And, I don't know how to say this, but it was calling out to me."

"I understand that feeling," Johanna said.

"He had pleaded with me not to go into the room, but I so desperately wanted that crate out of our house. I was going to pick it up, walk outside and dump it in the canal." She stared at her hands. "But I had to get close to it first. As I came closer to the table, I told myself I was not going to look inside. I was going to put the lid on. The lid was on the floor, leaning against the table leg. I crouched so that the bottom of the box was out of my view. The inside of the box was lined with red velvet, I could see that, and I was wondering what sort of thing justified this luxury. But I didn't look. I crouched to pick up the lid. It, too, had red velvet on the inside. I turned it over so that the velvet faced the bottom, and I held it in front of my face so I couldn't see into the crate. Apart from the red velvet lining, there was also something like a gold staff with a ruby on top. I could see that. I thought that wasn't such a bad thing to look at, but I promised him that I wouldn't, so I kept the lid in front of my face. And then I bumped into the table because you know I couldn't see where I was going. The golden staff thing fell over and the ruby hit something that made a dull hollow sound." She shivered visibly.

"And you looked."

"I looked. A black thing, a bit bigger than a man's fist, lay on the velvet. It was a bit bumpy and round on top and it was this round part that the staff had hit. At first I couldn't make out what I was looking at. It was dark in that room, and black is not the usual colour you'd expect . . ." Tears welled up in her eyes.

"Not the colour you'd expect what to be?"

"It was terrible. As soon as I looked at it and I realised what it was, I saw these . . . these . . . horrible visions. This girl screaming and screaming like an animal. A man with a knife, cutting her. There was blood dripping from his hands, on his clothes, even in his face." Greetje covered her face with her hands. Her shoulders shook. "I couldn't stop the visions. I couldn't stop her screaming, I couldn't stop him slashing at her. I could feel her pain."

She took a few fast breaths.

"And then I was yanked away. My husband was yelling at me at the top of his voice, saying all these horrible things. Holding me with my back against the wall. I screamed that I *had* to go back into that room. I was trying to get out of his grip, scratching his arms. This was when he hit me. I've never seen him so angry . . ." She cried in big racking sobs. Her shoulders shook. Her whole body shook.

"What was the black thing in the crate?" Johanna asked when Greetje had calmed down a bit.

"It was . . . it was . . . a skull of a newborn child." She started crying again. "It could have been our child! Murdered. With rubies stuck in the eye sockets."

Johanna held Greetje, waiting until she calmed down again.

"At the time when the Church of the Triune came to Saardam, there was a Belaman Church monastery in town."

Johanna had heard about that.

"Apparently, the abbot took a liking to deflowering young girls and would keep seeing these girls as a part of their repentance for whatever minor disobedience they had come to confess. Whenever the girl became with child, the monks would hunt her down and kill the girl. They would sometimes cut out the child to make sure it died. Apparently one girl managed to escape the monks until the day her child was born. The babe drew one breath before her head was chopped off and the mother cut to pieces. That is the skull of the child in the crate."

"And it's a church relic?" That was horrible. Disgusting.

"After this happened, a lot of people took to the streets and burned down the monastery and chased the monks out of town. The Church of the Triune gained a good deal of influence because of this. And because the newborn girl had drawn a breath, she became a ghost. Murdered people often become ghosts. No one murders young children. They're the most horrible powerful ghosts. Demanding, crying, powerless in anger. The church kept this skull to protect the citizens. My husband has been seeking ways to destroy it. I was so stupid to undo all his work. I should have listened to him. I'm not worthy of him."

"Come on, now. It's not easy to withstand a thing of evil magic. Even the best magicians have trouble with that." Johanna put a hand on Greetje's knee. "He will have to accept help. We'll talk to him tomorrow."

Greetje nodded, although she still looked scared.

Johanna rose. "You look exhausted. Go to sleep now. We'll talk to your husband in the morning."

Greetje leaned back in the pillows. She looked so pale and tired that she would probably be asleep very soon. Johanna also had a feeling that her pains would start before morning.

CHAPTER 15

JOHANNA WAS RIGHT about Greetje. Nellie woke her up when it was barely light, sneaking into the linen cupboard in the room.

"What?" she whispered.

Roald was still asleep. Nellie put her index finger against her lips, so Johanna rolled out of bed and followed her into the hallway.

"The pains have started," Nellie said. "Helena should be here soon."

Johanna went into the dressing room and got changed into her housedress. Her hands were sweaty with nerves while doing up the buttons over her own swollen stomach. Guess she was about to find out what was going to happen to her in late summer. The child mocked her by doing somersaults inside her.

Greetje sat on the rug in the middle of the room on her hands and knees. She didn't look up when the door opened, but let her head hang forward. She still wore the nightdress that Johanna had lent her. The fabric was thin, and the light that came into the window showed Greetje's body under the dress. Her belly was round as a water bag ready to burst. She moaned softly and rocked from side to side.

Nellie had dragged a little table into the room where she had lined up neatly folded towels and swaddling cloths, clean sheets, a jug of water, soap, and a little white gown.

The fire blazed in the hearth, even though it wasn't particularly cold.

Helena came in, lugging the bare wooden birthing chair that Johanna had sometimes spotted her carting through town. She plonked it on the rug next to Greetje, who eyed it suspiciously. Bare and made of dark wood, and with no seat except a narrow ledge, it looked like a piece of torture apparatus.

"Sit there," Helena said, after she put down her other things in the corner of the room. Johanna thought she spotted knitting needles and wool.

Greetje heaved herself up, wincing. "Do you want anything off?"

"Just the underthings. Leave the gown on."

Greetje sat on the chair, moving gingerly. The only way to sit on it was with her legs spread and it was not very elegant. Helena knelt on the ground, feeling under Greetje's gown.

Greetje gasped. She let her head hang forward, breathing deeply. She let out a soft moan.

Helena sat back and waited for the pain to pass.

Johanna involuntarily placed her hand on her own swollen stomach. It had tightened into a hard ball.

Greetje met her eyes. "I'm sorry. It really hurts."

"No need to apologise," Johanna said. She sat down in the single chair in the room. Her stomach had relaxed, but now she badly needed to use the outroom.

Helena asked a bit about when Greetje's pains had started and how often they came.

Greetje had to stop talking a few times, but it seemed a

quiet affair, not the frantic screaming that Johanna had heard other women talk about. If it was like this, she could handle it.

Helena climbed to her feet. "It's early days. This will take a good while. I don't know that it's necessary for you to sit in the room. Maybe ask a maid to check in with me every now and then. Have breakfast, do your normal things. I will call when there is progress."

Johanna nodded.

"Do you want me to bring some tea?" Nellie asked.

Helena said that she did, so Nellie left with Johanna. The cool breeze through the corridor made her shiver.

"Phew, it was really hot in that room," Johanna said.

"It's to keep out the bad air," Nellie said. "We don't want the little one to catch a cold."

"Do you think you can still go out and get me those pieces of wood that we were talking about yesterday? The longer we leave it, the more irrelevant images the wood will store."

"I'll do that right after I've brought the tea."

"Thank you, Nellie."

"You go and have breakfast."

Johanna didn't feel like it was fair for her to eat while Greetje suffered, but on the other hand if she didn't eat anything herself she would faint.

She found Father and Roald at the breakfast table talking about frogs. Or at least Roald was talking because Johanna had no doubt that Father had heard Roald's story many times before.

She sat at the table and ate a few pieces of bread and jam while listening to Roald. He *still* wasn't eating, so when there was a little pause in his story, she deposited half her bread on his plate.

"Eat it."

He stared at her as if the fact that you were supposed to

eat at the table was a new notion. "What about you? You have to eat."

"I will eat later." The few bites she'd taken of the bread sat uncomfortably in her stomach. Eating more was not going to help.

"I heard rumours that you didn't go to church last night," Father said.

"No, I was busy, forgot the time and was too late. I went to light a candle for Auguste LaFontaine."

Father raised his eyebrows. "Different church?"

"It was the right thing to do. I'm not sure that I agree with how much influence the Church of the Triune wants to have over the royal family. I think we may need to step back a little."

"That took you long enough to realise," Father said.

Typical for Father, he kept changing his mind about why he disliked the church. It seemed he was determined to dislike them no matter what they did.

"The church did many good things for common people at a time that they needed it." She thought of Greetje's horrid story about murdered girls. "They're still doing good things. They give people food."

Father said, "They buy souls with every food package they hand out. They shouldn't be feeding the people, the royal family should."

"What with?" She spread her hands.

She was starting to feel really ill and excused herself from the table just in time. By the Triune, women had told her that this sickness was meant to let up once your stomach started growing. Her body clearly had different ideas.

After a quick rest, Johanna then had to go to the kitchen, where the cook gave her some cake and soup. Halfway through eating that, Nellie came in again.

The cook asked her, "Do you still want to boil the water? It's been boiling for a long time now."

"Put it aside. She's going to be a fair while."

"How long?" Johanna asked, feeling chilled.

"Helena says it's very slow. No need to hurry to the guest room. I'm about to go out to run your errands, Mistress Johanna."

Johanna sat at her desk but succeeded at nothing more than staring at the letters she had been writing before the King's Council so clearly dismissed her. She thought of going to see the shepherd, but he could do nothing until the child had made its appearance. She went to have a look in the guest room. Greetje lay on her side in the bed, moaning, while Helena sat knitting. Nothing much happening there.

Johanna wandered to the guard station to ask how they were going with the investigation. Anton was on duty there and didn't seem to have much to do.

He told her that Auguste LaFontaine's body had been delivered to the family. The guards had spoken to the young man's family and friends.

"There is something going on with those people that he's friends with," he said. "We'll have to ask further when they're more amenable to speaking to us, after the funeral."

"Do you think they know more than they're telling you?"

"Certainly, but they're pretty protective of each other now. Their versions of events line up far too perfectly. We can loosen them up later. They have weaknesses we can explore. They're a bunch of raucous young men with none too good a reputation, if you get what I mean."

Johanna had to think of Nellie and her "these men don't say what they mean" speech. She guessed that "none too good a reputation" meant that the young men frequented whorehouses.

"Is Octavio Nieland one of those friends?" she asked.

"Octavio wouldn't call himself a friend of a bunch of young louts like that. They're more like his lackeys."

He didn't have much other news, so Johanna went to her office. The pile of draft letters mocked her from the corner of the desk.

It said to her *Look at you, little queen. You had notions that you could escape the fate of so many women before you. You thought the men would listen to your ideas. You thought that they would give you power. But whatever you do, you'll always still be a woman and they will never, ever take you seriously.*

She picked up the pile and leafed through the names.

Everything she did was pointless. Baron Uti, King Leo and King William wouldn't even know who she was. They'd say "The consort of WHO?" And they'd laugh and laugh.

She might as well throw the whole lot in the fire. Let the men do whatever they wanted. Learn to knit and sew and make pretty newborn outfits. Hold tea parties for the noble women. Admire their dressed-up brats. And grow roses.

After all, that was all Queen Cygna had done. No doubt she'd been a fighting spirit once, too, in her youth in the northern country where she had grown up. Maybe she'd dreamt of having her own fishing boats. One day, her father would have told her she was to marry a prince in another country. She would have cried, but she would have done as her father ordered, because that was what good girls did. After all, he was a prince.

Tears came to Johanna's eyes when she thought about it like this. In all the talk about the tragic circumstances of the royal family, Queen Cygna was rarely mentioned.

Nellie came to her room later in the morning. To Johanna's question about Greetje, she said that there was not much progress.

She carried a basket from which she dug a couple of items made from wood: a wooden spoon from the kitchen in the armoury and a twig from a broom in one of the quayside warehouses that belonged to one of the noble families of interest.

"It's quite hard to find things made out of wood that are small enough for me to carry," she said. "I don't know if these are any good. There are also a lot of people around, and I have to be careful."

Johanna had to smile when she imagined Nellie snooping around and *stealing* a wooden spoon from the armoury kitchen.

The spoon showed her a good view of the cook going off at a kitchen hand while soldiers lined up with their plates. The language was . . . interesting.

The broom twig was the most informative, except the broom had been in the broom cupboard and the images included a glorious view of the inside of the cupboard, while two male voices spoke in the main room. They spoke about nothing interesting—warehouse space—but the way in which they referred to her as "the little queen", as if she were a child, disturbed her.

"I'm sorry if they're not very good," Nellie said.

"It's all right. I didn't expect any of these pieces of wood to tell us precisely what we want to know. That would have been crazy coincidence. We'll probably have to go a few times while he guards are doing the formal questioning."

Nellie looked in her basket. "I swear there was something else. There were some wood chips from the saw mill." She rummaged in the basket and found the wood chip: a chunk of willow wood that looked to have been separated from the block with an axe.

In fact, the blow of the axe was exactly what Johanna saw when she put the splinter on her hand.

She winced.

Nellie said, "Oh, mistress Johanna, are you all right?"

Johanna saw a group of young men fighting on the sawdust-covered floor in the sawmill. No, they were play-fighting, laughing and being silly. They were probably drunk.

One young man had taken off his shoes and he carried another over his shoulder through the warehouse. That young man was yelling at him and pummelling his friend's back with his fists.

The one carrying his mate was Auguste LaFontaine. He flung the other man off his shoulder into the sawdust. His friends pounced on him with a slate sponge, covering his face in chalk. There was much laughter and silliness.

By the Triune, how drunk were these men? It was embarrassing to watch.

"Mistress Johanna?" Nellie asked.

"Yes, this is a good one." Johanna put the wood chip on the table. "Get me more from there and perhaps the quay outside."

Nellie nodded and left the room. She looked happy, and Johanna couldn't bear to tell her how pointless it all was.

CHAPTER 16

JOHANNA SPENT MOST of the afternoon on the couch in the living room. She felt tired and ill, and her feeble efforts to do some embroidery didn't come to much. Even Nellie was surprised about it when she came in to bring tea.

She nodded at the work on Johanna's lap. "That's an unusual sight, if you don't mind me saying so, Mistress Johanna."

"I thought, since it's my child, I better start taking an interest in the things that an expectant mother is supposed to do."

"Oh, but myself and the other girls can do all that. Just you keep busy with important things."

Johanna sighed. "They don't want me, Nellie. They're not going to listen to me. Roald is not going to turn up to meetings and help me. I'm tired of fighting these stupid, pompous noblemen."

"Just have a good rest. Your body is working very hard. No wonder you feel listless."

But Johanna felt it was more than that. She just thought

that by giving up her freedom and marrying the prince no one wanted to marry, she expected at least *some* people to be grateful for saving the royal family. But in truth no one cared, at least no one who had any power in Saardam.

So instead she found herself in this gilded cage without real supporters beyond Father and Master Deim, and without friends.

Later in the afternoon, a courtier came into the room. "I'm sorry to disturb you, Your Majesty, but this arrived for you." He carried a roll of parchment held by a white ribbon.

A silk ribbon, tied in a neat bow. The stamp in the sealing wax depicted a tiny dragon.

Johanna sat up and took it from him, her heart thudding. She broke the seal, pulled the ribbon and unrolled the parchment.

At the top was another dragon, this one hand-drawn in exquisite detail, by Li Fai's mother, Johanna guessed.

Underneath, it said,

To Johanna, esteemed Queen of Saarland.

She had to laugh at that.

The letter continued,

I appreciated your previous correspondence. The palace guards have been to our ship, and I am confident that they have seen the truth that we had no involvement in the poor man's death.

I have also noted your interest in the arts. I have asked my mother what can be done for a person who has grown up without a box. She has shown me some things I would like to try. If you're amenable, we could arrange a meeting in a mutually agreed place.

It was signed Li Fai.

Johanna held the letter to her chest, breathing its unfamiliar perfume. The eastern people didn't seem to have any customs that resulted in women being disregarded. They even wore trousers. Maybe she should hide on board the ship when it, inevitably, left Saardam for Anglia.

It was a silly thought. Of course she would never leave Father, but just the thought that no one on Li Han's ship raised any objections about Li Han's wife travelling with them made her own situation sting even more.

She cast her feeble attempt at sewing aside and went to the office.

In reply to Li Fai's letter, she wrote,

I would very much like to have a meeting. Magic is not taught to children in Saardam, since only few have it. In my limited travels, I have searched for people who could teach, and have never found anyone willing to do so. It is perhaps unwise for you to come to the palace in the current climate, and inappropriate for me to visit your ship, but we could meet at my father's office at the quay. Let me know if tomorrow two hours after midday would suit you.

Surely Greetje would have had the child by then.

She rolled up the letter, sealed it and went to the guard station to have it delivered.

Next, it was time for the evening meal. Nellie didn't show herself and neither did Helena, so Johanna ate quickly and went to the guest room to check on the progress there.

Greetje lay with her eyes closed on the bed. Her shoulders went up and down with deep breaths. She looked asleep, but probably wasn't. Helena was asleep in the chair, leaning back with her mouth open. Johanna didn't want to disturb either of them, so she left the room quietly. She'd best go to bed early. Most likely, she'd probably be called in the middle of the night.

But when Johanna woke up with a shock, it was to light streaming in through a crack in the curtains. She jumped out of bed, flung on a dress and went to the guest room.

Even before she entered, it was obvious that the birth had not yet happened. Johanna had quietly hoped so, but she could hear Greetje's distressed cries in the hallway.

By the Triune, this was the part that women spoke about. Her voice barely even sounded human anymore.

Suddenly scared, she hesitated with her hand on the door handle. Her stomach was tight like a rock. Her breasts tingled so much that it almost hurt. But she knew: this one thing was inevitable and she would have to go through it herself. She should face it.

The guest room was dark and hot. The curtains were drawn, the windows closed so that no evil spirits could come into the room.

It took Johanna's eyes a while to get used to the darkness despite the candles on the table and the mantelpiece.

Greetje sat on the birthing chair, stark naked and panting noisily. As Johanna shut the door behind her, she started crying again, an inhuman kind of *uuhh—uuhhh—uuhhhh* that made Johanna want to clamp her hands over her ears. It lasted a good while, then Greetje leaned back, her swollen breasts heaving with her deep breaths.

Johanna sat down next to Nellie on the corner of the bed.

Helena wiped Greetje's face, which shone with sweat. Her hair hung in sweat-soaked strands along the sides of her face.

In the moment of relative silence, Johanna whispered to Nellie if she wanted her to do anything, but Nellie said, "When the little one is out yes, but not right now. I've got the water on the stove. To be honest, it's been there all night. Helena says that it will be a while yet."

Did that mean she was going to scream worse?

So Johanna sat on a chair in the corner, while Greetje started crying again, and Johanna's stomach tightened and her breasts tingled.

It was as if the child inside her reacted to another mother's agony. As if it wanted to play, too. Johanna put her hand on her stomach. It even felt hard. She broke out in sweat.

A maid came to bring tea, but Johanna let hers sit on the

table next to her, afraid that anything she drank would come straight back out.

Helena took a quiet moment to gulp some tea and eat a piece of cake.

"Is she still all right?" Johanna asked. She *had* to distract herself from her panic. Her child was not ready to be born yet.

"First one is always very hard," Helena said.

Well, thanks for that. Johanna felt even sicker. The child inside protested with a volley of kicks in he stomach.

Greetje started crying again, so Helena abandoned her tea.

If Johanna had thought that the agony couldn't get worse, she'd been wrong. The pains came quickly, one after another. Greetje screamed so much that she grew hoarse. Helena made her drink water, but she threw up almost immediately, all over herself. She hadn't eaten for more than a day, and most of it was stringy yellowish slime. When Helena tried to wipe it off, she screamed obscenities such as Johanna had never heard a woman use, certainly not one who was married to a man of the church. She managed to get herself out of the chair and stood in the room stark naked, bruised, her hideously swollen stomach out of proportion with the rest of her body, crisscrossed by bright red stretch marks. She yelled that she wanted it to end and she didn't want to die. The tears were running down her cheeks.

Helena ordered her, "Then stop crying and start pushing. You're ready."

"I can't."

"You have to."

"I can't! It hurts."

Helena grabbed both her shoulders and pushed her down on the chair.

Greetje protested. "Ow, you're squeezing me."

"Then listen." Helena's voice was intense. "You're going to push like you've got to shit, and it's a really, really hard and big one, and you can't get it out. It's stuck down there, but you've been sitting on it for a few days and it hurts so much that it can't wait any longer. It's going to take a long time and it will hurt, but you push, and push until you're red in the face and your eyes go red. You push because if you don't shit, you die."

"Ew. How crude."

"That's what birth is like. It's crude. It's hard. It's messy. It's painful. If you don't do it, you die. So you push your guts out! Come on. Close your eyes and when the pain comes, push, push, push!"

Greetje closed her eyes, and when the pain came, she pushed, first carefully.

Helena kept shouting, "Harder! Like you have to shit. And you have to get that shit out of there."

Greetje went red in the face.

And again and again. She held her breath while pushing, going red in the face, and then let it out with an explosive sigh.

Again, and again and again.

Not making much progress.

Johanna now grew aware of how hungry she was. She eyed the remains of the cake, but decided against it and drank some cold tea. And coughed it back up.

Nellie gave her a concerned look. "Are you all right, Mistress Johanna?"

"I think so." She *hoped* so. The child was kicking her in the ribs. It almost hurt.

It was so, so agonising to watch, and it took so long, and Greetje's strength wilted to the point where she could not push anymore. She didn't even cry anymore, but drifted off between pains.

Helena cast Johanna a worried look. "She's ready but the child is big and sitting high and she's exhausted. I think her body is giving her a rest before giving it one more try."

There was a really morbid undertone in her voice. *One more try* was going to be the last try.

All of a sudden, it was too hot, too stuffy, too scary in the room. Johanna *had* to get out of there. She slipped out into the corridor.

The light outside hurt her eyes. It was now afternoon and golden sunlight slanted in through the windows.

She briefly went to the kitchen to get something to eat. The cooks were already preparing the evening meal, and the kitchen smelled of hearty soup. She forced herself drink some tea and walked around aimlessly, feeling sick and sweaty and afraid. If she didn't eat so much, then would her child be smaller?

When she came back into the room, Greetje's pains had started again. She trembled all over and was crying. "I can't do it, I can't, I can't. It's my punishment from the Triune, for being dishonest to my husband."

"That's rubbish!" Johanna was surprised at how angry she got. "I'm going to tell your husband that he's going to stop preaching that rubbish about not being good enough and taking up arms against the enemy as redemption."

Helena instructed Johanna and Nellie to each hold up Greetje between them. "I hope a change in position will make the child fall into place. It's still sitting too high. She needs all the help she can get."

Johanna and Nellie heaved Greetje off the chair. She was very slight and not heavy, even with the added weight of the child. Her arm on Johanna's shoulder was clammy and her muscles trembled. Helena instructed Johanna and Nellie to keep a good hold on her while she placed one of Greetje's feet on the back of the birthing chair and the other the arm rest of the other chair so that her knees were bent, her legs spread wide and Johanna and Nellie held her entire weight. When a pain came, Johanna could feel all of Greetje's body tense up. She'd push, she'd let out a loud *uhhhh, uhhhhh, uhhhh* like a mortally injured animal.

The pains rolled on relentlessly. There was almost no rest between them. Johanna felt deeply ill.

She was afraid and with each pain she became more terrified. She had to hold on tightly to Greetje's arm because she was drenched with sweat.

She pushed, screamed, panted, howled, swore, pleaded.

This had now lasted for the best part of the day and Johanna could feel Greetje's strength ebbing. It was not going to happen.

Johanna was doing none of the hard work, but even she was starting to feel tired with the effort of holding onto Greetje's sweat-drenched shoulder.

Helena showed no sign of giving up. In fact she was starting to encourage Greetje again. She shouted at her when she let her head hang for too long. And Greetje pushed and swore and howled.

Helena dropped to her knees. Both she and Greetje were screaming. Helena at Greetje, Greetje out of pain. Nellie started yelling, too, "Come on, come on!"

Johanna hoped that this was over soon, because she was going to throw up.

Finally, finally, something happened. A little head emerged, covered in wet hair. Helena helped ease out the child from between Greetje's legs. From her position, Johanna couldn't see it very well, but the face was all scrunched up. The body was pale and waxy and looked like something dead that had been in the water for too long. When the child was free, a gush of blood and mess came out.

There was a moment of intense silence. Helena's hands

holding the child were covered in blood. Was it too late? Had it taken too long? Johanna couldn't help but think of the child's skull in the box. Her vision wavered.

Then the little mouth opened and uttered a weak cry.

"Oh, by the Triune," Nellie called out in relief.

Johanna and Nellie lowered Greetje onto a towel on the bed. She was shivering and crying. "It was so terrible. I'll never, never do that again."

Her legs were covered in bruises and slick with blood. Her belly was floppy, the skin wrinkled. Her chest was covered in red blotches and her eyes were shot through with blood.

"Calm down, it's over," Nellie said. She dipped a washcloth into the boiled water which had long since gone cold, and started washing the muck off Greetje's lower body. Then she dressed Greetje in a clean nightshirt and tucked her in bed. By this time, Greetje's eyelids were drooping.

Johanna shivered. Her dress had gotten wet with birth fluids and felt disgusting and cold around her ankles.

Helena had wrapped the child in a cloth which made it stop crying. "Hey, hey, it's over. Look. It's a little boy."

She put the child into Greetje's arms, but Greetje was barely conscious and didn't even have the strength to hold it. Or to smile. Her eyes were half open, unfocused. Her face was more grey than pink. Her hair still wet and stringy from sweat. Her cheek was still blue from the bruising. The birth had lasted more than a full day and Greetje was utterly spent. She didn't want a boy. She didn't want anything at all.

It was not a happy occasion.

There was much cleaning up to do in the room, and Johanna helped Helena and Nellie. Nellie took the child to the next room, giving the boy a tender look. He was quiet. His face was red and swollen, his head bumpy and eyes gummed shut. He was ugly, to be honest, nothing like the cute little ones that Johanna had seen whenever she visited friends. He had suffered as much in the process as his mother had.

There was no cot, so Nellie had made a bed in one of Loesie's baskets. "I think I might ask a wet nurse to come for today," Nellie said. She stroked the boy's head.

For the thousandth time that day, Johanna wondered why she had ever wanted to have a child.

"That was not particularly pretty," Helena said, coming into the door.

"Is she asleep?" Johanna asked.

"Yes. She'll need bed rest for ten days. I'll come back this evening to make sure he's feeding properly. After all this, I'm exhausted, too."

"This is not how it normally goes?" Johanna felt somewhat relieved.

"I was about to think that we were losing her when she finally managed to push the child out. She is small. The child was big. It happens. I'd be dishonest if I said it will be easier for you. It may. It may not."

Johanna felt ill.

She knew that each time a woman became with child, she was tempting fate. It was not for nothing that Master Deim had made her sign documents that made Johan Delacoeur the regent in case something happened to her. The risk was so great. Her own mother had died while with child.

She decided: she would have this one child as heir for Roald—she didn't care whether or not the child was his—and then she'd find herbs that women in Florisheim were said to use to stop having children. Maybe, too, Roald would lose interest. That would be great. No more horse riding while having something big stuck up her private parts.

At any rate, she'd seen enough of this childbirth business to last her a lifetime.

IN JOHANNA'S DREAMS, she lay on her back with her legs in the air. Nellie was screaming, but Johanna was puzzled why. Helena sat on the couch knitting a huge sock, saying that she wouldn't do anything if there wasn't any tea. Roald was in the room, too, and he was saying that he couldn't possibly look at her with all these people in the room.

Johanna knew she was supposed to feel a lot of pain, but she didn't. Still, she knew she was expected to scream, so she did. She woke up with a shock, her heart thudding and her stomach tight. Her mouth felt dry. She hadn't *really* screamed, had she?

Sunlight flooded the room and Roald was gone from the bed.

Johanna rolled out of the bed and opened the door to the hallway.

Nellie just happened to be walking past. "Oh, there you are."

"You didn't come to wake me."

"I did, but you were fast asleep so I thought I'd let you rest."

Johanna didn't feel rested. In fact, she felt more tired than she had going to bed. "How is Greetje?"

"Still sore and tired, but the boy is feeding well."

"Has anyone told the shepherd about the birth?"

"A guard went out this morning."

"Where is Roald?"

"In the garden."

Everything was under control. Not even a dead body could keep Roald out of the garden for long.

Johanna went into the dressing room, followed by Nellie.

Nellie told her about how she had the baskets ready to go out to the LaFontaine and Nieland families.

She put a basket on the dressing table. From inside, she took a little woollen blanket, a tiny singlet with the letters ML embroidered on it, and three napkins.

"What is ML?"

"Josefina LaFontaine's little one is called Marie. I'm sorry for taking these things from your cupboard, but I can make some new ones before the child comes."

Johanna nodded. She was in awe of all the things Nellie did. "Do you ever sleep, Nellie?"

"Not as much as you do at the moment. But you need it, so don't worry about me, Mistress Johanna."

Nellie didn't even understand why Johanna was asking. "I also got the wood you asked for," she continued while doing Johanna's hair. "I've put it in your study on the desk. To be perfectly honest: I didn't get it, but I asked one of the groundsmen because he wouldn't look so much out of place in those warehouses."

"There's no need for you to get into trouble about this, Nellie."

"What trouble? He was glad to help. People support you more than you give them credit for."

Did they support her as mother of the heir to the throne or as someone who could help fix this broken town? That was the big question.

"Don't look at me like that, Mistress Johanna."

"Like what?"

"You don't believe what I said. I can see that in your eyes."

"It's not so much that, Nellie, it's that I think they want me to be a quiet little queen who wears pretty dresses and holds tea parties."

"I don't think they want that at all."

"But you want it."

"Mistress Johanna, whatever makes you think that?"

Nellie's eyes were wide.

Because every time I want to do something that's different, wear a different dress or create a fuss, challenge the church or whatever, you tell me not to.

But she let it rest. Nellie *did* support her a lot.

Johanna went to the kitchen for breakfast. The cook brought her porridge with cream and jam, and for the first time in days, she felt well enough to eat all of it.

She then went to her office where Nellie had left two little boxes. As instructed, Nellie had put a little note with each. One box contained wood chips from the sawmill, the other another twig from a broom from the warehouse where Li Han's ship lay moored.

The wood chips showed her the same young men, including Auguste, hanging around while one of their mates was working at a bench chipping away at a block of wood.

He put his hammer and chisel down. "Finished."

He showed his mates what he had been making, but

Johanna couldn't see that from the position on the floor where the wood chips had been.

The other young men appeared impressed. "You roll the paint on like this." He dipped the wood block into a paint-soaked cloth and stamped the block onto someone's arm.

Auguste yelled, "Hey!"

He held out his arm. The stamp had left a black shape of a dragon. "Hey man, what are you doing?" He rubbed at the spot but the ink didn't come off. "Look at it. I'm supposed to go out to dinner tonight."

"Do you think it's good enough?" one of his mates asked.

Another said, "If it stays on his arm, it has to be. He's the most slippery bastard in the entire kingdom."

His mates laughed, but one remained serious. "I don't know. It's definitely similar, but this one lacks in workmanship, so that when all the bags stand next to each other, he will be able to tell the difference right away."

"Are you criticising my whittling skills now?"

"I say it's good enough. We only want the stuff to pass the harbour master's inspection. It will be good enough for that."

His mates all agreed.

Johanna withdrew her hand from the wood chip. Well, *that* was interesting. She rose from the chair and went to the guard station. The guards were unfamiliar with her wood magic, so she had to talk in general terms. She made up that Nellie had heard rumours when running an errand to get something from Father's office. She also couldn't give the names of the louts, but *Auguste's group of friends* would probably yield those names when they asked around.

The guard frowned at her. "Some kind of illegal importing racket?"

"That's the rumour. And they've falsified Li Han's stamp to make it look like whatever they're bringing in is coming in under his name."

"That's disturbing. Any idea what sort of goods they might try to smuggle?"

Johanna shook her head. "I don't even know how much of this rumour is true."

"But we will surely check it out." His expression cleared. "Oh. By the way, someone brought this for you." He grabbed something off the shelf in the guard station and held it out to her.

As soon as Johanna saw the rolled up parchment with the white ribbon, she knew what it was about: she had completely forgotten about yesterday's meeting with Li Fai.

Oh by the Triune.

She took the message into her office where she broke the seal and pulled the ribbon with trembling hands. She unrolled the parchment.

It said,

I hope this finds you well. I have been informed of your condition and assume that this was the reason that I didn't see you at your father's office. I remain interested in meeting you. If you are well enough, please let me know a new time.

Johanna cringed all the way through reading this. How could she have forgotten about this? This was important. How *dumb* could she get?

What to do now?

Johanna pulled out a piece of parchment and her pen, and wrote,

Please accept my apologies. I will explain when I see you two hours after midday today at the same place.

She rolled up and sealed the parchment and went to the guard station to have it delivered.

CHAPTER 18

AFTER THE MIDDAY meal, Johanna told Nellie that she wanted to go out.

Nellie had just taken delivery of the first of the dresses that Mistress Dina had made for Johanna. This particular one was dark blue. Being made of velvet, it was also warmer, which was a problem, because the day was sunny and bright, more summer than spring.

Father stood at the door to his quarters when she left. "That dress looks even more 'proper' than the grey one."

"Does it?"

The sleeves were equally long, the neckline equally high and the top equally shape-less.

"I take it you're going out?" Father said.

"Yes."

He nodded.

"You're not even asking where I'm going?"

"I trust it's some place where you can do important things for the country. You're big enough to look after yourself now. I trust you won't get into trouble."

This made Johanna hesitate. Why *was* she in such a hurry to see Li Fai?

Yes, she didn't want to give his father reason to pull up anchor and go to Anglia.

Yes, she had never met anyone who'd been willing to teach her anything about magic.

Why did Father's question made her feel guilty, as if she was doing something untoward?

Father spread his hands. "But mostly, I've learned that whenever you're going somewhere or doing something, when you have it in your head that you want this, I can yell at the Moon for all I like, but you don't listen. And you know, it used to scare me, but I've also learned that whatever you do, you might not do in a way that I would have done it, but it turns out all right just the same."

Johanna laughed. "Well, that's a profound bit of wisdom on such a nice sunny day." Yet, the conversation chilled her.

She was far too keen to see Li Fai, and if she wasn't careful, it would lead to rumours. That wouldn't be so bad if only the rumours were true.

She continued into the foyer and down the steps, where the driver waited seated atop the coach holding the reins to the two white horses.

Johanna climbed in, assisted by a guard, and the coach set off.

Inside the luxuriously-appointed cabin, Johanna stared at the empty bench opposite her. Li Fai had sat there when he explained about his magic box. The little dragon had gambolled over her knees while she sat in the same spot as she sat in now. She could still see Li Fai sitting opposite her, with his very serious face.

No one else had ever talked to her about teaching magic. She had spent so much time in Florisheim looking for someone. The books in the monastery, her visit to Magda, none of them had ever told her what to *do* with magic.

As soon as she saw Li Fai's dragon box, she had wanted a box with a tree.

That was the crux of the matter. Nothing else.

Of course Johanna arrived at Father's office early. The coach dropped her off at the steps. She pulled her cloak about her shoulders while climbing to the front door.

It didn't look like anyone had been here since her fumbling with the ripped dress. Father did most of his work from the palace these days.

The first door on the left led to the official reception room. It contained two couches and a chair, a low table and, around the walls, bookcases with glass doors. The room looked tidy, but so much dust had collected on the seats of the couches and the table that she it would be embarrassed to use it. Father never used the reception room much, even when he still came here every day. It was too formal, he would say. The room had a window that looked out over the street, which made it unsuitable for holding this meeting. If Li Fai was going to do magic, she didn't want to take the chance that people might see it.

Father's office was at the back of the building and more suitable. She opened the door to air the room, but realised that if she wanted a fire in here, she should have come earlier.

It was not to be helped. She went back to the reception room. The coach had gone. As per her instructions, it would wait around the corner.

She eyed the people on the quay. Couldn't see Li Fai.

If, a year ago, someone had told Johanna how she would be looking at the quayside activities, she would have laughed. As queen? With child? The *Lady Davida* burned? An iron ship in the harbour?

Had there ever been a time, back then, when mooring

spots at the quay were unoccupied? When you could see substantial stretches of water in between the ships?

The wreck of the *Lady Davida* was somewhere on the bottom of the harbour, Adrian's watery grave. Father was still talking about building a new ship, but everyone wanted new ships. The shipyard had trouble getting wood, because people had a greater need for houses. It would be a while before the harbour filled up again.

Now she spotted Li Fai. He was coming down the quay in the company of one of his mountainous guards. Workers unloading ships and fixing fishing nets barely glanced at him. So much for a hostile reception. He even greeted one or two of the workers.

He came up the steps to the front door. The knocker fell on the wood.

Johanna went to the hallway to open the door. Li Fai bowed.

"Do come in." She wasn't sure what to say to the guard, but he seemed to assume that he'd wait outside.

Johanna closed the door, shutting off the sounds from the street. "I'm sorry about yesterday."

"You are well?"

"I was not the problem. Someone . . . close to me was . . . unwell." It seemed inappropriate to go into too much detail. Johanna could still hear Greetje's screams and they still made her shudder. "Let's go to a more comfortable room."

She preceded him to the office. Coming here with a visitor would of course mean that she should sit in Father's chair. The tall, heavy chair with the leather-covered seat almost swallowed her. But the velvet of the dress had as much grip on the shiny leather as shoes on ice.

She straightened her back. "Well, uhm . . . ." This was awkward. All of a sudden, she realised the wide variety of political rumours that might start if people knew she was here with him. Planning behind the King's Council's back, consorting with the enemy, using evil magic.

He dug in his pocket and placed two boxes on the table. One was the octagonal dragon box she had seen before. The other was plain. The wooden polished surface gave no indication of its contents.

He didn't need to say that the box was hers. The wood sang out to her.

"Can I touch it?" She held up her hand.

He covered the lid of the box with his hand until she withdrew. "We give a box like this to a child to store their art. The box itself can be either just a pretty thing or very significant. If it can be made from the same material that the gives the child their art, then it makes the art more powerful. The art of wood is much-coveted around the known lands. It might not be spectacular and might take a long time to master properly, but its power is infinite."

Johanna looked at the other box with the little dragon on the lid. She felt like protesting. *But . . . Dragons!* Yet every single person who knew more about magic than she did always told her the same thing. *Wood is stronger than fire. Without wood, there cannot be a fire.* Even Loesie had said this.

"I don't have the art of wood and I don't know how this box would work for you. It is not exactly the type of box we would use for children, but we have no children on board and have no reason to take those boxes. This is a simple box of the same wood. My father had it in his cabin."

"This isn't just normal wood, is it?" None of the type she was familiar with anyway. Most of the lid was straw-coloured, mottled through with flecks of brown and red. Yet the surface was polished smooth as glass. The wood's fibres shone like silk when the light fell on it at a certain angle. In the surface of the lid, the direction of the wood's grain changed in two places, giving the impression that the lid was twisted while it was perfectly flat. It was a curious thing.

Li Fai continued. "Wood artists tell me that different types of wood have different strengths."

Johanna nodded. Willow wood was best of the wood types she knew.

But she also knew without touching the box that it was made from a type of wood much stronger than that.

"This wood is from a pine tree that grows on top of the world in mountains so high that the slopes are a wasteland of broken rocks and snow. The trunks are usually split and stunted, and instead of growing straight like normal trees, they twist over the ground, sometimes trying to rise, like a creature rolling on the ground in a terrible sickness. The trees fight the icy winds that come to its home from all over the world. They drink the rain and snow that fall from the clouds that float over all the lands. The trees are ancient because they grow very slowly."

"That sounds like a very wise type of tree."

He nodded. "People with the art of wood do not touch it lightly. This wood has a very long memory."

She understood, and shuddered at the thought of the stories such an old and wise tree would have to tell.

"But you must touch it, if the box is to become yours."

She reached out again, but he grabbed her wrist. "No, not yet." His expression was serious, and made her feel like she had almost done something extremely dumb.

Johanna withdrew her hand, still feeling the warmth of his touch on her wrist.

He rose from his chair.

In the corner of the office was a table where Father tended to put things that came from the warehouse. It contained a messy stack of bags and lengths of rope to tie them. He pulled out a couple of the ropes.

"I'm sorry I have to do this, but it's for your own protection."

He crouched next to her and tied a rope around her leg and the leg of the chair. He tied a knot in the rope.

"Hey, what does this mean?"

"Again, my apologies. People can have very strong reactions to the wood. There are stories of people having jumped up and injured themselves. With young children, a parent usually holds the child on their lap, but if I did that, you would not find that appropriate." He glanced at her while tying up her other leg.

She was trying to decide if he'd meant it as a joke. His face remained completely serious.

Then he knotted two lengths of rope together. He looped this around the backrest and to the front.

"Not too tight. I'm with child."

"I know."

His fingers were soft-skinned and gentle. The rope was rough. The words were on her tongue, *Look, I'd prefer if you held me.*

Appropriate it was not, but some part of her didn't care about what some stuffy noblemen considered appropriate. She wanted to feel the dragon magic and see the little dragon again.

He rose. "I'm leaving your arms free. You can wave them around, but I'll stand far enough back so that you can't reach me."

Johanna felt chilled. "This is not going to harm the child, is it?"

He inserted his fingers between the rope and her dress. "It's not too tight." The back of his hand brushed her dress.

Johanna took in a sharp breath. She was going to say, "Hey!" but a stream of magic went through her that made her entire body tingle. Whatever magic that was, she didn't see any images, but she could feel them.

The call of the wooden box on the table.

The sighing of the wind around the building.

The slapping of the water against the quay.

The straining of the little dragon inside the other box, butting its head against the lid to get out.

The keening of Alexandre's spirit trapped inside the tree.

The cramped struggle of the child inside her.

All those things combined into a big throbbing vein of magic that coursed through her body.

Li Fai's dark eyes met hers. "The child has the art and it's at least as strong as yours."

That's because the child is Kylian's. Sweat broke out on her back.

He withdrew his hand.

Then he turned to the desk and picked up the plain wooden box. Johanna held her hands up, her heart thudding.

He held the box a hand's width above her palms. "Understand that the great power of this wood is not that it shows the past. It is that it shows possible futures."

He lowered the box in her hands.

Johanna's vision went dark.

CHAPTER 19

GHOSTLIKE FIGURES emerged from the darkness, hazy at first. Johanna had to blink her eyes a few times before she could see properly.

She was in the church, in a pew about halfway down the back, a place she might once have occupied when she was simply Johanna Brouwer.

It must be night, because the little windows near the ceiling were dark. The only light came from the candles that burned in sconces along the walls and on the pillars that supported the roof.

She was standing and all the people around her were standing, too. Johanna didn't recognise any of them.

At the sound of a bell, a procession of people started making its way down the aisle to the front of the church. They wore long dark robes that covered their heads and hid their faces.

No one in the regular church services wore those robes. Not even at funerals. And what were they all doing here? The service usually only involved the shepherd and a few altar boys.

The person at the front could be the shepherd. Maybe, maybe not. He was tall enough to be a man, but walked with a limp, like an old man. As he passed Johanna's position, he turned to her, but she still couldn't make out a face inside the shadow of the cowl, only the faint glint of an eye.

A draft of wind tore through the church, ruffling bonnets and hair.

It chilled her to the core of her body, but no one around her reacted.

"Hey!" she said to the woman next to her. She just sat passively staring into nothingness. Her face was pale and her eyes didn't move. For a moment, Johanna thought that she was surrounded by dead people, but then the woman blinked.

"Hey!" she said again, but the woman didn't react.

The procession slowly made its way to the front of the church. The first man climbed the steps. From within his robes, he withdrew a bundle of red cloth and laid it on the altar.

The cloth crumpled to the table, except for one lump about the size of a man's fist.

All the members of the procession now stood in a half-circle behind the altar, except the man who had carried the parcel, who leaned on the altar as if his back pained him. His hands were pale, the fingers thin. Some of his fingertips looked strangely dark.

He lifted his hands and pushed back the hood. The man's head was bald, his eyes deep within their sockets. His nose was thin, his lips dark and his cheeks sunken and scabbed.

But even if he resembled a walking skeleton, Johanna recognised the shepherd, Master Willems.

With trembling hands, he pulled back the red cloth. A gust of wind almost tore the cloth from his hands. It buffeted the windows, rattled the doors. A tiny door to the side of the altar that led to the bell tower creaked open and then slammed shut.

The blackened skull underneath looked even eviler than when Greetje had described it. The two rubies in the eyeholes glowed with ghostly red light.

"Behold the evil that attempts to invade our city!" The shepherd's voice was shrill. "It has taken many of us already. It has taken three altar boys, it has taken my housekeeper, my wife and son. I have tried in vain to protect you from it, but I cannot do this alone. We must sit on our knees and pray. Oh holy god, I place this terrible thing before you so that you can smite it before the eyes of the people, before it destroys all that is dear to you."

At the front of the church, a woman started crying. Johanna leaned sideways so that she could see who this was. To her great discomfort, she recognised herself.

Alone, no longer with child.

A cold feeling took hold of her. What terrible thing would happen that made her wail like this? What would happen that made the people of Saardam sit quietly and watch their queen cry without a single sign of emotion? That would allow her to walk up to the altar in the middle of a service to face the skeleton-like men in their long robes? To accept a hammer from one of them?

She turned to the altar.

That child's skull? That was the child she carried. Conceived in that place of dark magic. Resurrected. Imbued with Celine's ghost. The *necromancer*'s child.

Johanna in the pew watched herself stand over the altar, hefting the hammer above her head. The glow from the skull's ruby eyes turned her face red.

The shepherd faced the congregation, raising his arms. His sleeves fell back, revealing just how skeletal he had become. His forearms were thin as sticks, his elbows swollen. A red rash covered his skin, with ugly sores and scabs.

"Believers of Saardam, today we bring to you the destruction of the evil that has plagued us for months. We have brought into our midst a former member of the church who went on to betray us, but who is the only person who can destroy this thing of evil: the mother of the necromancer's daughter. Go now, smash this evil and let us live in peace without magic."

Johanna at the altar brought the hammer down.

The black skull shattered. Fragments flew off the dais, some landing on the steps. One of the rubies bounced to the shepherd's feet.

A deep male voice laughed.

And laughed.

For a few terrible seconds the congregation was as quiet as death. Everyone stared at the fragments of the shattered skull. Johanna was just beginning to think that it was over, when the fragments started to crumble, and crumble, and turn into fine black dust that *oozed* over the red velvet like slime. The trails joined to form blobs and bigger blobs.

The shepherd gave a strangled noise. The ruby that had landed at his feet had melted into a red jelly. The glob crept towards him like a headless slug.

A woman at the back of the church screamed, "There, there!"

She was pointing out the open church door.

A white ghost drifted in, followed by another and another. People screamed, trying to push away from the aisle, even if the ghosts paid no attention to them. They made for the shattered relic. Johanna near the altar could feel the icy air as they passed, and melted into the ever-growing blob of slime.

More ghosts came in a frantic rush. The shepherd's cup

and staff, standing on a shelf behind the altar, were yanked from their places and absorbed.

And then a man close to Johanna in the pew bellowed an incoherent shout. As he opened his mouth, a cloud of mist flew out, over the heads of the congregation, and joined the blob. The man fell face down on the bench.

A woman—his wife probably—rolled him over. His eyes were wide open. The irises had gone white.

She started screaming.

Similar screams also went up elsewhere as more and more trails of mist were sucked into the growing blob. People tried to run, were struck by the invisible magic and fell where they stood. Others tried to climb over the growing piles of bodies, only to be struck themselves.

The blob grew and grew, extending tentacles outwards, picking up bodies in its hunger for living souls.

It grew into a structure that resembled the ugly algae-covered growths that sometimes washed up on the shore. A red glow throbbed within, like a giant heart. With each beat, the structure grew and grew. Its tentacles now reached for the roof of the church, frantic, probing. It pushed at the windows up there, dislodging panes of glass. It reached onto the roof. Its heart throbbed so hard that the air vibrated with it. *Whoop, whoop, whoop.*

It was still sucking souls, mostly coming in through the door of the church or the broken windows. Each soul made the thing grow, made the heartthrob louder.

And then with one last *WHOOP*, it exploded.

Johanna ducked between the pews. Dust and debris flew over her head.

When she looked up again, the roof of the church was gone. The shepherd and the hooded men who had come with him lay like desiccated skeletons on the floor.

Now most of the noise came from outside.

Johanna made her way to the door of the church as quickly as she could, stepping over debris and arms and legs of dead people. Clouds of smoke blew through the church, and from somewhere behind the altar came sounds of wood popping in flames.

She stopped at the top of the steps.

All of Saardam was on fire. The houses along the market-place, the palace, the remaining warehouses along the quay, even the few ships that had survived the previous fire, even Father's sea cow barn.

She ran through the streets strewn with bodies to the harbour.

The flames reflected in the still water of the harbour, in the place where Li Han's iron ship now lay. A chain of men was passing up buckets of water to the quay while others ran to and fro from the quayside to a burning building, tossing their futile efforts into the roaring flames.

The king's armoury!

Johanna wanted to scream at them, "Get out of there!" but she had no voice.

As she watched, the roof of the building burst open and a fireball bloomed from the inside. Debris flew outwards.

The men abandoned their buckets and ran.

Too late. The expanding explosion engulfed them.

One jumped off the quayside, but the flames licked his back in midair. He fell into the water, a burning figure, and did not come back up.

From the fire emerged a vaguely human shape that, as it walked over the quay, resolved into a man. His clothes were on fire, his hair was on fire, but he kept walking as if that didn't bother him.

She recognised his face: Alexandre had broken free of the tree that had trapped him. Someone else emerged from the fire behind him. Kylian, his orange hair trailing flames.

He laughed, and pointed at Johanna.

A sharp pain tore through her body. Johanna clutched her stomach, to find that she was yet in another possible future and the child was still inside her.

"What are you doing?" she gasped.

He laughed. His hand leaked fire, which he casually flicked at Johanna. It danced over her stomach. Another lancing pain tore through her.

"I am with child!" she gasped as soon as she could speak again.

"As if I didn't know that."

"Then be careful."

He laughed.

"It's your child."

"I know that. It's time for the child to face the world."

Johanna gasped with the pain. She stumbled back until she hit the wall of a house. Stood there gasping. She could feel the child's head pressing between her legs. It burned like fire. Something wet ran down her legs and when she shifted, she left bloodied footprints. The child was going to kill her.

She screamed and screamed.

"Hey, hey!"

Johanna bent over, gasping, clutching her stomach.

"Calm down, calm down," a man's voice said.

Li Fai's face swam into focus. He was looking at her with an expression of concern.

She was still on the chair in Father's office. Pale sunlight slanted into the window. A pigeon crooned on the roof.

"Oh!" Johanna gasped, and burst into tears. "That was the most horrible thing I've ever seen." She cried with relief. She was safe. There was no fire. The shepherd was not a walking skeleton. The relic was whole. Her child was unborn. Greetje and her son were alive.

Everything was all right. For now.

Then she looked up at Li Fai. "You're saying that this wood shows the future?"

"Possible futures."

"But that's horrible."

"Then you must take steps to prevent those futures. Are you all right?"

"Yes, I'm all right. I think." She was still catching her breath. A ghost of the pain lingered in her stomach.

Prevent those futures, he said. That was easier said than done. Many girls before her had tried to rid their bodies of children that had taken root. Many had died in the process. But if she would die giving birth anyway, then surely it was better if the necromancer's child died with her?

She felt sick. Sweaty, trembling.

Li Fai knelt at her feet to untie her legs. Wherever he touched her, his magic sang in her veins.

She set down the wooden box that she still held in her hands.

She said, "Li Fai."

He looked up, his perfect eyes meeting hers.

"I need your help."

"I'm always happy to teach."

"No, please. I need your help. Your dragon. Your magic. We need it badly."

The ropes that had held her feet were now undone, and he moved behind the chair to undo the knot that held the rope around her body.

She swallowed hard. "The child . . . I don't think it is the king's. The crate you brought for the shepherd contains a newborn's skull. It's a horrible church relic. The shepherd just said. . . ." She had to stop to compose herself. "He said that I was the mother of the murdered child resurrected. The father . . ." She sobbed. "The father of the child is an evil magician. A necromancer. He plays terrible games with people. This child is a resurrection of the murdered child whose skull is in the box."

"How does the shepherd know that?"

"I don't know. He's the shepherd. He knows things like this." Johanna hid her face in her hands. "He is also a magician." What else could she have done to prevent this? She'd been doomed from the moment she danced with Kylian. The moment she first laid eyes on him. The moment he kissed her.

If only she hadn't listened to Father and hadn't gone to the ball. If only Roald was able to father a child. If only she hadn't been so keen to come to the Guentherite farm where she had witnessed Kylian's necromancy, and where he had bewitched her.

But what would she be, except dead many times over, if she hadn't done any of those things?

She met Li Fai's eyes. "Please. Do you have anything, magical or no, to get rid of this child? It's evil."

Li Fai pulled her up.

Johanna rose so quickly that blackness encroached on her vision. Whoa.

"Careful!"

A pair of hands steadied her. Li Fai had to use all his weight to stop her falling. When she had regained her balance, he said, "Evil is rarely born. It is made, through lives lived in deprivation and lack of opportunities or learning. If I may?" His hand hovered over her stomach.

She nodded.

He laid his full hand on the swelling. His eyes widened briefly. Johanna's heart jumped.

He said, "The child's art is strong. If you teach her well, she will be a good queen."

But Johanna hadn't missed that first reaction, that brief expression of horror that confirmed her deepest fears.

"I can't have this child!" Tears leaked out of her eyes over her cheeks. "I have to get rid of it."

"We have herbs that stop a woman from becoming with child. We have magic that expels a child that has just started growing. We have nothing that can stop a child growing once the woman's belly has started swelling."

Johanna cried, in big sobs. "I don't know how to teach magic. No one teaches magic in Saardam. No one has magic. Please, help me."

He gave her a stern look.

"About three years ago, when my family was in Lurezia, we met an astute businessman who had a very successful river trading business. My father liked this man a lot. He bought an awful lot of my father's goods, far more than any river trader did. When my father asked this man why he did so well, he said that he had a clever, hard-working daughter who did a lot of his dealing with buyers, making sure that accounts were paid on time, and who would have ideas that made a big difference to the business. For three years, I looked forward to meeting her."

Johanna fell quiet.

A deep shame crept up in her.

What had happened to that Johanna Brouwer? Why had she let the King's Council push her aside? Why hadn't she sent those letters about the investment in the port of Saardam yet? Why had she been afraid of a bunch of pompous, huffing and puffing nobles?

Because they don't listen to me.

A voice, sounding like Master Deim, responded in her thoughts. *Then you must make them listen, child.*

Johanna wiped her eyes with the back of her hand.

Li Fai was still looking at her.

"I'm sorry, I . . . let myself get carried away. I swear you can still meet that merchant's daughter."

Ho nodded. "I will look forward to that."

She knew what she must do. She had been wrong to let the King's Council have their way. Wrong to try and remain polite.

She grabbed her cloak off the backrest of her chair.

"You're leaving?" Li Fai asked. "You haven't even opened the box."

True. She held out her hands as he gave it to her.

She braced herself for another onslaught of images when she touched the wood, but this time the vision was gentler .

The box took her to a sun-filled meadow with flowering buttercups. The sky was blue, but the larks were no longer singing. The trees were still green, but autumn was in the air. Johanna lay on the riverbank, watching the water flow past the waving reeds, while willow fluff drifted on the air. Her feet hurt from carrying her and her hugely swollen stomach from the jetty that she could see in between the willow trees. Saardam lay on the other side of the inlet. The church tower poked out of the jumble of houses.

Li Fai sat next to her. He had ditched his armour and his black clothing and wore a simple white tunic and blue trousers, such as Saardam's merchants would wear. His hair was loosely tied in a ponytail. He held a parchment on his lap that contained a map. New canals, streets, an entirely new part of the city which would be built right here, after they built a bridge over the creek.

But right now, he rolled it up, bent over her and gently kissed her lips.

Johanna yanked out of the vision, heart thudding.

And Li Fai in Father's office was looking at her with the same intensity.

He smiled, oh so innocent. "You were in such a hurry to get out. Open the box."

Johanna did. A puff of dust blew out. It whirled and

shaped itself into strands and thicker strands. It formed a miniature trunk with real bark, and little branches and tiny green leaves.

She laughed. "It's a willow tree."

"It is your art. Carry it with you always. You can call on it when you're in need. Do know that this is only the start."

"Will you teach me more?"

"Where I can."

His gaze was so intense that it made Johanna's ears glow. *Possible futures* were really no more than that, were they? Images borne of wishes and fears. They did not necessarily become true, did they?

Johanna slipped her cloak over her shoulders. "Those horrible things I saw in the wood will not happen. I'm going to stop them from happening. I will write letters to all the royal families and other people interested in the port so that we can stop future wars. I will go to the shepherd and demand that he accept help in destroying the church relic. When my daughter is born, I will teach her not to become like her father."

He nodded at her. One corner of his mouth moved up a fraction.

CHAPTER 20

JOHANNA HAD STAYED away much longer than she had expected. It was now time for supper before getting ready for church. And she was going to church tonight. She was going to confront the shepherd, and was not going to back down.

In fact, she wasn't going to take no for an answer ever again. She had asked Li Fai to come to the church as well. If what they were facing was as bad as her visions had indicated, then she would need him badly.

In the dining room at the palace, she found Father and Roald at the dinner table. Father had the stack of letters and the draft plan on the table. For a change, Roald seemed to be listening.

Johanna sat quietly on the far end of the table, and ate while watching Father explain the plans that they had prepared and that had so skilfully been thwarted by the King's Council.

He explained about the investment allotments which anyone could buy for warehouses and other necessary structures to be rebuilt. He explained about the warehouses and offices.

It was *her* idea and her plan, but Father was doing very well at keeping Roald's attention, so she simply listened.

Johanna could see it now. If they were successful, there would be a need to build a bridge across the creek and build warehouses on the land on the other side, where she and Li Fai . . .

Her ears glowed. Just *thinking* about this was inappropriate. She should stop this while she still could. Her current situation was bad enough.

But those eyes . . .

And his singing magic.

And the little cavorting dragon.

And all the things he knew that she had never been taught before.

Including how to completely, utterly, hopelessly fall in love.

That realisation shook her. It was silly. It was stupid, impossible.

But many royals had mistresses and secret lovers said a little voice inside her. It was not that she didn't love Roald. She did, like a brother. And it was not as if he'd shown much interest in her in that way recently.

She stared out the window, her chin leaning on her elbow, while Father exhausted Roald's willingness to listen to the plans.

After dinner she asked for Nellie to see her in the dressing room. She came in carrying a stack of clean nappies which she put on a shelf. "That boy sure knows how to dirty his bottoms. He has a good set of lungs on him, too."

"Has she named him yet?"

Nellie shook her head. "She's still wondering why her husband hasn't been to see her."

"Maybe because he has other things to worry about?"

Nellie gave her a sharp look. "I haven't heard that tone in your voice for a long time, mistress Johanna."

"Welcome it back."

"Did anything happen?"

Yes. I fell in love. "No. I'm sick of waiting for those stupid men to solve my problems. I'm done with being polite. I don't think I'd ever be much good at embroidery and knitting."

"No, mistress Johanna."

"Is that a statement of criticism?"

"It's the truth. Also, if you ask me, mistress Johanna, things get awfully boring around here if you try to be polite."

Was that honestly a smile in Nellie's eyes? "Anyway, Nellie, could you do my hair?"

"Are you going to church tonight, mistress Johanna?"

"I sure am."

So it was done. Not much later, Johanna made her way down the palace steps to the waiting coach.

It was only a short ride to the church, but it was busy in the market place and the driver had to ring his bell several times.

Johanna alighted from the coach at the bottom of the church steps. Many people were going up the church steps and filing into the doors.

Johanna walked down the aisle and sat down in her pew at the front. She looked over her shoulder. Li Fai had also arrived. He even stood talking with the old farmer who complained that sitting hurt his backside.

It looked like the service tonight would be well attended. She spotted some women with little gifts. Likely the news about the shepherd's son had gotten out.

Behind the altar, two boys were lighting candles. One of them carried the big *Book of Verses* to the altar and opened it at the right page. It was that same altar where, in her vision, Johanna had shattered the skull.

She shivered.

The boys were ready with their preparations and took up position at the back.

They waited.

And waited.

Where was the shepherd?

"He should have been here by now," Johanna said to Anton.

"I don't know, Your Majesty."

People at the back were also getting restless. Some half-rose and glanced at the door—which remained open and empty. The altar boys had trouble standing still. One of them was nervously shifting his weight from one foot to the other and back again.

Johanna rose and gestured for the boy to come down the steps. "Do you know where the shepherd is?"

"No, Your Majesty."

"Did he say he was coming?"

"He didn't say that he *wasn't* coming, Your Majesty."

"Will you run to his house and see if he has fallen asleep?"

"Yes, sure, Your Majesty." He ran out, his tunic with tassels flapping.

There was a sound at the door, and voices. A moment later, the boy came back in the company of Shepherd Carolus, who strode down the aisle towards Johanna. His face was red and his straw-like hair even more dishevelled than normal.

"Oh, You Majesty, you must come. Something is going on with the shepherd."

Johanna rose, her heart thudding. This was it.

She and Anton followed the Shepherd Carolus down the

aisle. Johanna gestured for Li Fai to come with her. He came, giving her a tiny comforting smile that warmed her.

She returned a polite nod, hoping it wasn't too formal, or too informal, or that it would start rumours. He was only a business contact, right? Only a friend.

He followed her into the coach where they sat on benches facing each other without saying anything.

When the coach stopped, Li Fai reached for her hand. His skin was warm and dry, in sharp contrast with her hands, which were cold and sweaty.

He said, "Hey. You will be fine."

Johanna nodded, trying to believe it.

"You saw the possible futures in the wood."

She nodded again. Out of the three possible futures she had seen, there was only one she wanted.

She began, "Li Fai . . ."

But now Anton came to the coach door and opened it.

The Willems family lived in a moderate house in a relatively narrow street that connected two main canal streets. This far from the palace, the fires had spared or only slightly damaged most of the houses. Because this area had a high concentration of church families, many of them had fled after the occupation; and while a good number had returned, the fate of many others remained unknown. Both Master Willems' parents had been killed by Alexandre's barbarians, and he and his young wife had lived in the house ever since.

It was not a lavish or large place. Dark curtains obscured the windows on the ground floor. On the upper floor, some glass panes were broken or missing, replaced by small pieces of wood. Someone had scrubbed the steps even if they hadn't been able to remove burn marks from the walls and servants' door.

Johanna went up the steps to the main entrance. She

dropped the knocker on the door and waited while Li Fai remained at the bottom of the steps.

And waited.

And knocked again.

The sound of voices drifted from somewhere. When she held her ear to the door, it seemed the sound came from inside the house.

She went down the steps to the servants' entrance.

Voices came from inside that door, too, and when she knocked—no knocker here—someone opened the door quickly. A young maid, whose eyes widened when she saw Johanna. She dropped into a curtsy.

"Oh, Your Majesty. You should have knocked upstairs."

"I did. No one opened the door."

"Oh." She put her hand over her mouth. "I'm sorry. Come in."

She followed the maid into a dim hallway with a very low ceiling, and through a side door into the kitchen. It was not as big or well-appointed as the kitchen in Johanna's house, and the ceiling was really low, making the room pokey and dark. A couple of pans stood on the stove and the cook was kneading bread at the table in the centre of the kitchen.

A couple of other maids and servants sat around the table. They all rose when Johanna came in.

"Sit down, Your Majesty," said the groundsman, still wearing his coat. He indicated the chair he had just vacated, with a sideways look at Li Fai.

"It's not necessary. I'm not staying long. I only came to see the shepherd. Shepherd Carolus came into the church to say that something was wrong with him."

The groundsman and the maid exchanged a dark glance.

"Yes, you may well be staying long," the groundsman said, his voice dark.

"What's going on?"

The groundsman shook his head. "No one is quite sure, Your Majesty, but it's not good."

"Can I see him?" Johanna asked.

They exchanged worried glances.

The groundsman said, "I'm not sure that's either a good idea or safe."

"I've got someone with me."

He glanced suspiciously at Li Fai. "I don't know that it would help much."

"Is he—forgive me for asking—but is the shepherd practising . . . magic?"

A few more uncertain glances.

"Don't know if that's the word, Your Majesty."

"Nah," the cook said. She hadn't yet spoken. She was a stout woman with ample breasts and broad hips. "The word you want is exorcism."

The maid exclaimed, "Anna, you don't say—"

"It's accurate enough," the groundsman said.

"Have you seen any evidence of . . . strange phenomena?" Johanna asked.

"Nah," Anna continued in the same blunt tone. "He just seems to think there are."

The maid protested, "You don't know—"

"Nah, I don't know anything," Anna said. She put flour-covered hands at her sides. "I'm glad I don't know anything about this stuff. And that I don't have to go up there to do any work."

Johanna's heart thudded. She felt that they knew more than they let on. "We're here to help him. I think he's been stubborn and has refused to seek help with this box he received."

At the same time as the groundsman said, "What box?" the maid said, "Greetje said it had been sent to him by the Holy Father of the Belaman Church. She said he wouldn't tell her what was in it."

Anna and the groundsman glared at her. They were, perhaps, under instructions not to mention the box that the shepherd told everyone he didn't have. Why did he think he could handle this alone? "I still want to see him."

"The young master is not in a state to speak reasonably," the groundsman said, his voice dark.

"I still want to see him."

He nodded, gravely. "Come."

He left the room and Johanna and Li Fai followed him. Anton stood in the hallway. He was too tall to stand up straight in this very low corridor.

"We're going upstairs," Johanna said.

"Do you want me to come?"

"Maybe stay close where you can come quickly if I call you."

He nodded, his face grave. Johanna often wondered what her guards knew of magic. It couldn't be much, but they had to know that she possessed it.

The stairs were at the end of the hallway and quite steep compared to the ones in Johanna's house.

About halfway, there was a little landing where the stairs switched back in the other direction. The only thing Johanna could see about the upper floor was that it was dim and dark.

The groundsman gestured. "It's the last room on the left. You will find it easily."

Johanna became aware of an eerie sound: first a slap like that of a wet cloth on stone and then a grunt. "What is that noise?"

"Trust me, you'll be sorry you asked that question."

CHAPTER 21

JOHANNA SLOWLY CREPT up the stairs, trying to be as quiet as possible. A couple of the risers creaked badly, but the noise upstairs didn't stop. In fact, now that she was closer, it became louder.

A slap followed by a grunt, slap, grunt, slap, grunt.

Li Fai followed close behind. His face showed little emotion. He held his hand in the pocket of his jacket where his dragon box would be.

Johanna carried her box in her handbag and wondered if she should take it out, too.

She stopped on the first step after the landing. They were now out of view of the groundsman and Anton but couldn't see much more of the upstairs corridor than a section of wall and the large grandfather clock that stood there.

The noise continued. *Slap, grunt, slap, grunt, slap, grunt.* It was nothing like she had ever heard before. The grounds-man's words still echoed in her mind, and with every step she became more convinced that she *would* be sorry for asking what it was.

Li Fai had stopped next to her. He extracted the dragon

box from his pocket. The dragon figure on the lid glowed with orange light. He was about to open it—

Johanna put her hand over the top of his hand.

He looked up and met her eyes.

How could she ever have thought that his face was unemotional? The expressions were subtle but that didn't mean they were absent: concern, alertness, determination.

A moment passed in which neither of them moved. Johanna wanted to say what the wood had shown her that *might* happen between them, but she didn't know where to start. She wanted to taste his lips before going to face the evil that might kill her, or him, or both of them. But all she could do was stare at him as his unusual dark eyes looked back at her.

She wanted to touch him, but was too scared that he might get angry. That he would be upset or, scariest of all, would remind her that she was married and that this was most inappropriate. That he didn't feel the same things she did.

Meanwhile that horrible sound continued upstairs.

Slap, grunt, slap, grunt, slap, grunt.

"We must go," Li Fai mouthed.

Johanna nodded, feeling the magic moment slip through her hands.

Li Fai went first, Johanna following close behind. Up the last flight of stairs, into the hallway.

At the very end of the hallway a door stood open. A glow of firelight came from the room, casting a rectangle of orange light on the floor and opposite wall.

Johanna and Li Fai edged down until Li Fai was almost at the rectangle of light and could see into the room. He beckoned Johanna over. She peeked past him.

The room was bathed in firelight. All around the walls, on tables and cabinets that held books and statues and other objects, stood candles with flapping flames. They were all church candles, too, representing a fortune in good quality wax.

The shepherd stood in the middle of the room with his back to the door. He had stripped the shirt off his upper body. It hung around his waist. Unlike Roald, he was quite broad in the shoulders. He held knotted ropes in both hands and took turns flinging each rope over the opposite shoulders and slapping it across his back. The ropes hit his skin with a wet slap, and each time, he let out a grunt.

His entire back was raw and bleeding, his hair loose and soaked with blood. Each time he flung the rope, a spray of blood flew from the soaked fibres onto the walls and floor.

The smell of it hung in the air.

Johanna raised her hand to her mouth, swallowing hard to keep the bile down.

She didn't think she made a noise, but he must have heard her because he turned around.

His face glistened with sweat. His chest looked no better than his back. Blood ran down his chin, down his neck and over his chest.

"What are you doing here?" His voice sounded raw.

"I . . . I'm sorry. I was going to . . . Why are you doing this?"

He took a few steps to the door. Johanna backed into the opposite wall. He bent over her and bellowed in her face, "What are you doing here?"

Johanna was unable to say anything except utter a tiny squeak. She was fighting to keep her dinner down and to keep the black spots from her vision. She was aware that something warm and glowing orange landed on her shoulder.

The shepherd froze and then backed away, staring at Li Fai's dragon.

"What are you doing?" Johanna asked again.

"It's a church matter."

"Beating yourself raw is a church matter?"

"It's none of your business! Why don't you go back to your nice palace and let me deal with this, huh?"

"Since when has it been all right to speak to your queen like that?"

The shepherd snorted, flung the ropes onto the table in the middle of the room and put on his shirt. Spots of blood soaked into the fabric at his back. His hands trembled while he did up the buttons.

"You received a parcel from the Belaman Church," Johanna said. The dark-coloured crate stood behind him on the table.

He gave her a *what?* look.

"It contains an ancient relic from the church that the Most Holy Father Severino returned to you, now that the Belaman Church has cast our church out."

"You don't have to tell me what it contains. I'm dealing with it."

"It is a thing of dark magic. How do you think you can deal with it by killing yourself like this?"

He said nothing, didn't move, didn't acknowledge her question. By the Triune, she was feeling terrible all of a sudden.

"Why hide it? Why pretend that you don't have it? Why not call for help?"

He just stared, his mouth twitching. Drops of sweat rolled over his forehead.

Johanna looked into the dimness of the room. Now that her eyes were used to the darkness, she could make out the vast collection of objects on the cabinets that stood against the walls.

A shelf contained statues of stone, clay and wood. Some

represented various forms of the Triune, others were single figures.

A velvet-lined tray contained jewellery made of silver. There were pendants, medallions and rings for fingers much bigger than hers with the Belaman cross, or skulls. Another tray had teeth and bones, and much-thumbed books that almost fell apart with age.

A soft red glow edged the rim of the open crate. Johanna had first thought that this was from the fire and all the candles, but now she realised that the light radiated from inside the box.

"That's it, isn't it?" she said.

He said nothing so she stepped past him into the room.

"Don't touch it." His voice sounded raw. "Don't look at it, in . . . your condition. Greetje . . ." His voice wavered. "Look at what it made me do! She sneaked in here when I wasn't looking, she let that terrible thing set its magic loose on her and our child."

"Greetje is fine," Johanna said. "Your boy is fine."

"Boy?"

"He was born yesterday. She had a very hard time, but she's much better today. She is wondering why you haven't been to her."

His eyes were wide, the whites shot through with blood. "Because I'm bewitched! Because I will contaminate her!" He was trembling so much that he could barely stand. "I can't see her. I need to destroy this thing first."

"Then accept our help."

The shepherd glanced sideways at Li Fai, whose dragon had returned to his shoulder.

"He's a magician."

"So am I and so are you. We are going to need magic to defeat this thing."

"Magic is forbidden by the church!" His eyes grew wide

again. "My great teacher the Shepherd Romulus always said that the world would be a peaceful place without magic. It was magic that killed him, magic that did all this to our town!" He spread his hands.

"Probably, but magic exists, and it's not going away. There is no point in denying it—"

"It is evil!" Spit flew from his mouth. He picked up the ropes and started hitting himself again.

Both Johanna and Li Fai jumped forward. Johanna made for his left arm, Li Fai grabbed his right side. He struggled, uttering a beastly growl.

The rope dripped blood over the front of Johanna's dress. Her hands almost slipped off his arm with his sweat.

She yelled at him, "Stop doing that! There is no point."

"I am evil. I am tainted, not worthy to be the Triune's servant."

Li Fai said, in his soft voice, "Evil is never born. It is made out of despair, poverty and ill treatment."

The shepherd blinked at him. His eyes showed whites on all sides.

Johanna said, "Calm down. It's this evil thing that has made you have these thoughts—"

"It's in the *Book of Verses*! This evil thing is a sign from the Triune, sent to me to demand my repentance." The sweat was dripping off his face. "It's . . . it's . . . a punishment for the times I've used the evil in me to my own advantage."

"So that's what it's all about? You're still denying your own magic?"

"Magic is a force from the Lord of Fire."

"Stop being so stubborn. Some of us are born with it. There is nothing in the *Book of Verses* that says all magic is evil."

"There is! It says in—"

"We'll have that discussion once we've destroyed this

relic. We cannot do that unless we use magic." She stepped sideways to pass him. He grabbed her arm. Johanna used the little trick that Kylian had shown her: she grabbed hold of his wrist with her free hand and twisted. Her arm came free.

"You cannot fight evil with evil. It's . . ." His eyes rolled back in his head. His knees buckled. It surprised Johanna so much that she couldn't hold on to him. He crumpled to the floor.

Johanna met Li Fai's eyes in a moment of horror. By the Triune, what now?

She shook the shepherd's shoulder. His hand flopped about. He uttered a low moan.

Well, that wasn't part of the plan. They were likely to need the shepherd's magic. "Come on. Wake up!"

Now she became aware of a low hum that made the floor vibrate. She met Li Fai's eyes. "What's that?"

Li Fai went to the table and looked over the rim of the box. As he did so, a red glow pulsed from inside.

Johanna gasped.

Li Fai jumped back. The little dragon on his shoulder shrieked and jumped into the air. It hovered over the box, hissing at its contents.

Red light pulsed back.

The dragon hissed again.

Red light flashed in response, stronger than the previous time.

"Can you stop it doing that?"

Li Fai snapped his fingers. The dragon snorted a puff of flames and came back to his shoulder.

"What can we do now?" Johanna shivered. She thought of the tentacled blob with the pulsing light inside. Was there even a way they could safely destroy this thing?

She was going to ask Li Fai, but he was staring at the shepherd. A pale mist surrounded his head.

A slight breeze wafted into the door and made the mist swirl in the direction of the table.

"No," Johanna said. That mist was his essence, and the thing in the box was going to suck it up, and become stronger.

She jumped in front of the misty tendrils, but they wound their way around her. Never mind destroying the relic, the first question was: how could she keep it from getting stronger?

Crude measures were needed. Greetje had said something about a lid . . . There it was, leaning against the wall. She ran a few paces across the room and grabbed the lid. Her fingers met with the soft fabric of the lined inside. She turned the lid so that side faced down, kept it between the red glow and her face, and slammed it over the top of the crate.

The red glow vanished from the room.

Phew. That was almost too simple. Li Fai blew out a breath.

"Give me something heavy to put on top." The lid hummed under her hands with the power of the thing inside.

Li Fai picked up the first thing within his reach: a stack of books, which he slammed onto the lid. The pale mist surrounding the shepherd's head had vanished.

Johanna crouched next to him, shaking his shoulder. "Shepherd, shepherd." She shook harder. "Master Willems?"

He groaned.

Thank the Triune, he was still alive.

But now she became aware that something else was happening in the room. The books that Li Fai had put on the lid had caught fire. Flames licked the leather covers and the corners of the pages. One of the titles was an abridged edition of the *Book of Verses,* the other two were also religious titles. Li Fai's dragon danced around, trying to stamp out the flames. Smoke blew from cracks between the lid and the crate. Li Fai had retreated to the door, his mouth open. The glow of the fire turned his face orange.

"What's going on, Your Majesty?" Anton had come up the stairs. He held his sword raised, but one look into the room and he resheathed it. He took off his jacket instead and flung it over the burning books. The dragon jumped on the jacket and it seemed to have put out the flames.

"Careful. Get out of here!" Li Fai called at him.

"Come on, get up." Johanna pulled the shepherd's arm. He was too heavy for her, so she yelled at Anton who was still staring at the dragon. "Help me take him out of the room."

Anton took the shepherd's other arm and they dragged him backwards to the door.

The crate was still blowing smoke from the cracks. The smoke smelled acrid and foul, like the burning of waste.

The little dragon was now trying to fold itself around the crate, closing off the gaps by putting Anton's jacket in front of the openings with its paws or tail. But there were too many gaps, and when something went *poof* inside the crate, the creature scuttled off to its master.

Li Fai held his dragon on the palms of his hands. He blew on its back, as if blowing out a candle. The dragon shivered. It glowed brighter. It *grew*.

A sibilant voice whispered in her mind, *Without wood, there cannot be a fire. Without wind, there cannot be a fire. Without fire, there cannot be dragons.* The voice sounded like Loesie's, but that was impossible, of course.

Johanna understood it now. That was the hierarchy of magics. Wood, wind and water were basic magics without which the others could not exist. In order to reach for the power of dragon magic, there needed to be wood to fuel the fire for the dragon to use. Without wood, fire, water and air, a dragon was nothing.

The crate was made of wood. Johanna had once made broom and shovel handles grow. Could she do that again?

Johanna opened her bag and took the box out. She had touched it so much last night that it barely still showed her possible futures. That future was now in her own hands.

The little tree unfolded itself when she opened the lid. A breeze sprang up and made its branches wave. It brought humid mist that made little droplets on the leaves, which ran down the trunk.

The tree grew a root over the edge of the box, and down over her hands and another one on the other side. Both roots reached the table one after the other. A third root wrapped itself around the crate, with side-roots creeping over the wooden surface. It secured the lid in place. The wood sprang little buds and bunches of pine needles. It grew and grew.

The lid cracked, releasing a gush of thick smoke. Red light pulsed within the depths of the box, two ruby-coloured eyes, accompanied by the *whoop, whoop, whoop* of the soul-sucking heartbeat.

Little flames sprang up around the gap where most of the smoke came out. They crept over the tree's bark in an ever-expanding patch.

The air whirled around, fanning the flames. Johanna had to do her best not to run. The smoke made her cough.

Something large and warm brushed past her. Li Fai's dragon had grown so large that it almost didn't fit into the room. It pawed the gaps between the tree roots where the smoke came. It held its nostril at a gap and exhaled with a gush of air. Flames leapt out the other side of the tangle of roots.

The relic hummed, and a flash of red light blew outwards. The dragon growled. Smoke trailed over the floor. The shepherd lay there, his eyes still closed. The smoke didn't touch him. The wind that whirled through the room kept the smoke away from him. In fact, the breeze was coming *from him*. It was the voice of his wind magic.

The breeze grew stronger and the flames grew bigger. The smoke curled up around the dragon's legs. The wind tugged at the smoke and when it didn't budge, grew stronger, and stronger, and stronger. The tree's branches waved. The roots still grew thicker, crushing the crate into an ever-shrinking space, which caused more smoke to come out. The fire grew and grew.

The dragon nosed it, blowing flames in and out of its nostrils. It inhaled, drawing in flames and exhaled, fanning them. Inhaled and exhaled. The fire roared. It inhaled and exhaled, and inhaled—

And all the flames were gone.

The wind still tore around the room, tugging at the smoke, but by itself, it would never get rid of all of it.

The dragon sat very still. It occasionally blinked an orange eye. When it breathed, a puff of smoke came from its nostrils.

Then it slowly lowered its head. It stuck its snout into a gap between the tree roots. It roared. A gout of fire spewed from its mouth.

Johanna screamed.

She retreated, but the growing tree had not only crushed the box, it had grown twisted and interlaced roots all over the floor. She tripped over one and fell on her backside, losing her grip on the wooden box. She could barely still see what was going on and could barely breathe.

A strong gust of wind tore through in through the door. It whistled in the tree's branches. It blew aside the curtains. The windows blew open. Smoke billowed into the fresh air, and dissipated into the night. The tree had enclosed the entire crate in a mass of twisted roots.

The wooden box lay at Johanna's feet, empty except for a few sparks.

"Close it," Li Fai said in the silence. He still stood at the door and didn't appear to have moved at all.

His dragon gambolled through the air, having shrunk to its former size. It jumped onto his arm. He scratched it under the chin while it held its head up.

CHAPTER 22

ANTON AND THE SERVANTS, as well as some people Johanna didn't recognise who might be neighbours, stood in the hallway, staring into the room. Several people gasped and uttered exclamations of surprise.

"What in the Triune's name is going on here?"

"Look at the tree."

"Oh, the poor shepherd."

"It's the Queen!"

Johanna heaved herself up, brushing dust off her dress.

Her fall didn't seem to have had any effect on her child. Women always said that you shouldn't fall when with child, but like so many of these warnings that old women loved to give people, that was probably a fable. Maybe she should try to ride a horse next.

The shepherd groaned, pushing himself into a sitting position. His shirt was soaked through with blood and stuck to his back. His hair hung down in dirty strings soaked with blood and sweat. But his expression was clear. He frowned at the mass of interlaced tree roots that covered the table and surrounding floor. The tree was a strange thing, made up of part willow, part oak and part pine.

Then he frowned at Johanna.

He inserted his hand under his shirt. It came away wet with blood. "What have I been doing?" He looked around. "What happened to my spare room? Where is Greetje?"

"She is safe."

His frown deepened. Then his face took on a horrified expression. "I want to see her. I have to apologise."

"Yes, but I have to talk to you first."

Johanna met his eyes. Then he looked down. His cheeks grew red.

"Wind magic," she said. She had strongly suspected for years, but had never heard it out of his mouth.

He nodded, like a little boy caught with his hand in the sweet jar.

"So much wind magic that it burst free of its constraints."

The shepherd said nothing. He had contained more than twenty years' worth of wind magic. That might be why he spent so much time here in this room and he had become so obsessed with dealing with the relic without any help.

"Because it finally broke free, we could encase this evil thing. I don't think it's gone. It's still there under the tree."

"I guess I'll have an interesting spare bedroom."

Johanna shook her head. "I wouldn't stay in the same house with that thing. Who knows when it is going to come back to life. You can come and live in the palace until we know what to do next." There were a good number of people there already. One extra family wouldn't make that much of a difference.

He protested weakly, "But this is my parents' house."

His parents had died in the fires. "It's not to be helped. You can return once the evil has been destroyed completely. Maybe it would have been better not to take the crate home."

"And have this evil thing in the church?"

It was telling that he considered the church, or his standing in the church, to be more important than his family.

"Do you know who sent you the crate?" She thought of what Li Fai had told her about the monk who didn't want to have his name recorded in the ship's log. It now made even more sense than it did when Li Fai said that it was common that senders chose to remain anonymous.

"Someone in the Belaman Church who hates us, who would be familiar with the power of this thing. I'm not convinced that the Most Holy Father Severino knew anything about it."

"Is it a known, proper church relic?"

"It's a relic of *a* church. The Church of the Triune doesn't hold much value in relics or other holy objects. This clearly demonstrates why. Objects are nothing. At most, they're symbols for the real thing."

Johanna knew differently, but clearly, the shepherd was not ever going to change his mind or his attitude towards magic. And to be honest, he had always been like that.

Not much later, Johanna took the shepherd to the palace in the coach with the white horses. He sat opposite her, where Li Fai had sat before, but the silence between them was cold. It was very late or very early, depending on your point of view, and she felt exhausted. The scent of fire and blood still hung around her.

She thought of all the times she had ached to speak to him about magic, and all the times he had either ignored her remarks or questions or had actively denied them.

With the box—Li Fai had assured her that it would grow a

new tree next time she opened it—she understood far more about magic than she ever had.

Not so long ago, she had even considered marrying Master Willems because of his magic. What a miserable marriage that would have been.

More miserable than her own marriage in the last few months? Of course she had not fought with Roald, but he had been unwilling to do anything she asked.

She should be more demanding, not take no for an answer. Same as with the King's Council, she should speak up and tell people how it was going to be done, not wait until they approved, because they never would.

She would write the letters and send them.

She would answer any questions they had, and lead the meeting when the leaders of countries and cities arrived.

If the King's Council had objections, she would address them, and then go ahead and do whatever she planned.

Johanna witnessed an awkward visit of the shepherd to his wife. Greetje still sat in the bed, although she looked healthy and happy. He seemed reluctant to hold his son, as if he was still afraid that he was contaminated, or that he would contaminate the boy.

She didn't think that the problems between them were restricted to what had happened with the crate. According to the servants, they had always fought.

While he went back home to collect some clothes and other items, Johanna went to her office. It was cold and dark in there. Her eyes were gritty with fatigue, but she lit a candle and, by its light, completed the letters she was going to send tomorrow. One to King Leopold of Burovia, to the regent of Lurezia, to Baron Uti, to the Aroden family, to King William, to Li Han, to the mayors of the major towns on both the Rede and Saar Rivers. The pile grew. She was going to face all of Saardam's enemies and make peace with them.

When she was finished with the letters, she wrote out more details about the investment plan. There was a meeting of the King's Council tomorrow, and nothing and no one would keep her from attending.

By the time she finished, the sky on the horizon was starting to turn light blue.

Johanna blew out the candle and walked quietly through the hallway to the royal bedroom.

She had almost reached the door when a dark figure came out of the shadows.

Johanna gasped. "Who goes there?"

A man's voice said, "Forgive me, I cannot sleep."

It was the shepherd.

Johanna blew out a breath.

"I'm sorry to disturb you at this time. Now that . . . I've acknowledged my . . . gift, I keep seeing things wherever I go. When my wife breathes out over my skin, I see her deepest wishes."

Ouch. In his case, that couldn't be anything except painful.

"I promise myself and her that I will do everything to make her happy. But she is asleep, so I can't talk to her yet. So I go and stand in front of the window, but the breeze from outside tells me stories, too."

"Hasn't it always done that?"

"Not like this." His voice was barely a whisper. "I've seen . . . on the wind . . . the Red Baron is coming. King Leopold is coming. King William is coming."

"I know that," Johanna said. "I've invited them."

A Word of Thanks

THANK YOU very much for reading *The Dragon Prince*. The story is not finished here! In book 6, The Necromancer's

Daughter, all stakeholders to the rebuilding of the port come to Saardam, and Johanna juggles their egos, disagreements and murder attempts.

As author of this book, I would appreciate it very much if you could return to the place where you purchased this book and leave a review. Reviews are important to me, because they help readers decide if the book is for them.

Also be sure to put your name on my mailing list, which I use to notify subscribers of news and new fiction. For every-thing else, please visit my website at pattyjansen.com.

ABOUT THE AUTHOR

Patty Jansen lives in Sydney, Australia, where she spends most of her time writing Science Fiction and Fantasy.

Her story *This Peaceful State of War* placed first in the second quarter of the Writers of the Future contest and was published in their 27th anthology. She has also sold fiction to genre magazines such as Analog Science Fiction and Fact, Redstone SF and Aurealis.

Patty has written over twenty novels in both Science Fiction and Fantasy, including the *Icefire Trilogy* and the *Ambassador* series.

pattyjansen.com

BOOKS BY PATTY JANSEN

MORE INFORMATION:

PATTYJANSEN.COM

www.ingramcontent.com/pod-product-compliance
Lightning Source LLC
Chambersburg PA
CBHW030627190726
48286CB00008B/2427